First Aid Seamstress

© 2021 Nadja Fernandes, Subiaco, Western Australia

Publication date February 2022

Cover illustration by Ingrid Weyne
Cover design by The Copy Collective Pty Ltd TA Red Raven Books
Typeset in Myriad Pro
Typeset & Layout © The Copy Collective Pty Ltd TA Red Raven Books
Level 2, 194 Varsity Pde, Varsity Lakes Qld 4277

Print on Demand, ePub

Fernandes, Nadja, author.
    First Aid Seamstress, Fernandes, Nadja
    ISBN: 978-0-6452967-1-6 (pbk)
    AND 978-0-6452967-0-9 (epdf)
    Subjects: Fiction, contemporary fiction, romance
    LGBT – Australia
    Discrimination – Australia
    Religion – Australia
    Families – Australia

A catalogue record for this work is available on request from the National Library of Australia.

NATIONAL
LIBRARY OF AUSTRALIA

First Aid
Seamstress

By

Nadja Fernandes

DEDICATION

To my beautiful daughter, Beth

Acknowledgements

I'd like to thank many people. First of all, Amelie Hintermeyer de Ostrov, who in a figurative way, gave birth to me, returned me to life, 20 years ago. Thank you also to Dr Susana Pedernera, who helped restore my faith in life. Thank you, Danielle Fernandes Alves, my sister, who always believed in my writing, being the first to read all of my texts. Thank you, Dad, for teaching me to see the invisible, to hear what was present in silence, and translate it using verbal language. Thank you, Mum for teaching me that although we are all flawed, there is value in each and every one of us.

Thank you also to my very dear friend Camila, whose knowledge of the medical field has been invaluable, as has her support and encouragement. Thank you also to Maria Aleuda Fernandes, my grandmother, who's been a fundamental role model in my life. Thank you, Kelly Macdonald for answering my random questions about Subiaco, schools in the '90s, etc. In fact I should thank the whole family, as you all have taught me something. So thank you Peter, Rita, Nat, Kim, Mischa, Charlie, and Eva. I'm particularly grateful for having been pushed down your front steps (joking), resulting in an injury (not joking), but also in a beautiful friendship.

Thank you, Claudia Lanyi, for your patience, especially dealing with my bad mood before I'd had my first coffee in the morning and thank you for the many coffees you made me years ago. Thank you, Andrea Ostrov, my 'sister-by-adoption', thank you "Gabi con i", my niece, and Gabriela Lema, my friend, former classmate, and highly skilled translator. Thank you, Bev, for patiently reading my many drafts, and I suspect this isn't one of your favourite genres. I love your work as an editor.

Thank you, Ingrid Weyne, who converted my idea for a cover into a tangible and stunning image.

Finally, I'd like to thank Beth, my daughter, who had to put up with my obsessive writing, especially between July and September. She had to endure not having as much of my attention as she wished for. Thank you, Baby! There's a book in the queue which will (also) be dedicated to you.

CHAPTER 1

WINTER

Winter again. Cold wind renews the morbid air of death that insists on visiting us every day, hoping to find a door open. Sometimes I hide from that chilly wind, unaware of the macabre intruder that follows me. Nevertheless, the strong scent of eucalyptus often entices me and helps to bring more balance, neutralising the atmosphere around me. I think of all this as I walk around Lake Jualbup, breathing the crisp air, fine as the blade of a dagger. I start running again. I want to exhaust myself. It's the only way to feel better.

I look up and see a great grey ceiling and am reminded of life, as I see a white bird taking flight, swinging her sumptuous wings. I slow down but keep moving. Somehow, I am able to watch it all in slow motion, as the dagger pierces my lungs, once, twice, a few times, until I feel there's a rope around my neck, and I'm choking. I keep thinking about that letter, the words echoing inside my ears, the letters being etched onto my soul, like carvings on ancient rocks.

I flex my knees, with my hands splayed on my thighs, head down. Then I sit on the ground, take my backpack off my shoulder, open it, and get my water bottle out. I feel tears forming, but I don't want it to be true, so I empty the rest of the water onto my face. I get up and try to run again, but I'm already exhausted. I give up at the sight of a log lying on the lush grass. Our rainy season has made everything green and healthy. I sit on the log and immediately feel my butt getting wet, but I don't mind it that much. Then I place each elbow on my thighs, rest my face on my open hands, and close my eyes until a dog brings me back to reality. It puts its two front paws on my legs and tries to lick my face. I smile, pat it, and hear someone call.

'C'mon, Buster. There's a good boy!'

And the dog runs away from me.

The feeling of choking has abated, and I am breathing deeply but slowly like my therapist has practised with me. The dagger is gone for now. Instead of a cold blade, I feel there is like a fire burning inside my chest. I get up again and try to take flight, then I remember my wings are broken.

To most, my scars are not visible. To me, they are a map which traces the places I have visited, especially the ones I should avoid at all costs. At all costs? Dominique says I'm wrong. Dominique says that sometimes we should go back. If it was too cold, then go back wearing warmer clothes. Too hot? Wear something light. Something like that. She reckons that it could help to deconstruct a negative memory and adjust it. Add to it. Not replace, but integrate.

She also thinks I can grow my wings again. She doesn't realise they weren't simply trimmed or pruned, but cut off. Amputated. All I have left is their shadow—the shadow of my wings.

CHAPTER 2

PLAY DATES

Felicity and I met a while ago. Years ago. It took me a while to get to know her, but it did not take long for me to realise she had the right name: 'Felicity' means happiness, and she represents that. I wonder if she is aware of that.

When we met, we both had children, and we both knew that our kids were our top priority. I feel that I was lucky to meet them, and the kids, mine and hers, get on so well. It's almost like they're our extended family, although I never said that to her, as she may not have felt that way, and she may have also thought that I was some weirdo back then.

Charlie and Lola. Just like in the cartoon. They're Felicity's children. Charlie is six now, Lola is ten. My twins, Rupert and Reuben, are the same age as Lola. They all go to the same school, although the ten-year-olds will be out of there by the end of next year. Then who knows?!

We only met properly because my car, my very old car, broke down and all of a sudden, I was taking the bus to kindy with my two kids, who were then four. It was a bit of a walk from the bus stop to the school, and Felicity spotted us one day and asked me what had happened. I remember looking at her beautiful dark copper ringlets of hair and wondering if the curls were natural. I never wondered about the colour, though. I always assumed that was her natural hair colour— and it was.

Felicity is about five centimetres taller than me. On top of that, she likes wearing high heels, so I often have to look up when standing near her and interacting. She's fit but not very athletic. She says she hates exercising. She's not the lazy type, though. In fact, she's quite active and physically strong. She likes being active but isn't into sports, nor is she a gym-goer. Neither am I, by the way, but I force myself to exercise, purely out of principle, like a commitment to myself. At times I've wondered if it is to punish myself. It's better to believe it's to look after myself.

She's an internal designer and loves fashion. If you enter her bedroom and open her wardrobe, you'll find a dozen bags and probably 25 to 30 pairs of shoes. I actually love her shoes, but I only own about ten pairs. That's counting my sports shoes and my thongs.

I'm not into fashion. I don't even think I understand fashion. If I do, it's in a very intuitive way. I do appreciate Felicity's stylish shoes and clothes, but they're just not my style. I'm comfortable wearing jeans and Converse shoes. In winter, I go for leather boots, but the last time I wore high heels was probably when I was still married to Adam. They just hurt my feet too much, so I suppose I prioritise comfort over looks.

I also love Fli's house. The wooden frame at the rear has huge glass panels that climb up and over the attic. It's wonderful to sit there at night-time, especially when the sky is clear and when there's a full moon. She uses that space as a special 'chill-out' room. It's furnished with a red couch, some cushions, a dark grey carpet and beige blinds.

Her bedroom is also very funky. To start with, her bed's round and huge. Of course, the kids love it, and why wouldn't they? But I've often wondered where she gets the bed linen from. I've always forgotten to ask.

On her bedroom walls, there are some modern-looking paintings. Behind her bed, there's a curved wall. To the right, you'll find her wardrobe, and next to it there are some white shelves; a bookcase actually, except that there aren't many books in it.

She was always very hospitable, helpful and accommodating, especially when it came to helping me with the kids. I did the same for her, but up to meeting her, I had not been able to count on anyone else in that way. Eventually, I decided to get an au pair to see if it worked. But by that time, Felicity and I had become closer and closer.

When I told Felicity about my work, she joked and said, 'So you're also an internal designer!' Not quite. I'm a counsellor, and I specialise in substance addiction and substance abuse. At the moment, I work twice a week at a correction centre, where I run regular workshops but also offer therapeutical services. The other days I work for a government agency. I don't work full-time and try to organise my hours in a way that allows me to be home when the kids are home. Felicity's joke was that I help people re-design their internal life.

Until my car broke down some seven years ago, we'd only met at school events or briefly before and after school. So I told her my car was getting repaired and she insisted on taking us home that day. Her car was so fancy that I was scared to get in. It had leather seats and a shiny dash with a glossy brown steering wheel. The floor was a bit messy, but that is the reality for most parents. Still, her car looked much nicer than ours.

'I'll pick them up tomorrow. You can come with us or just stay home. Up to you. Just bring your booster seats for the boys. I'll leave them set up for as long as you need.'

At first, I felt grateful, then as time went by and I still did not have my car back, I started feeling embarrassed. She was very skilled in putting people at ease, and I was no exception. I don't know how she managed, but it was almost like she always had a smile tucked into her pocket or somewhere. Whenever you were worried, she'd pick up that smile, put it on and offer it to you, along with some wise, gentle words, and then you'd realise everything was okay, even when it was not.

All this was before I moved closer to the school. I had decided to enrol my twins in that school, despite the fact that I did not live in the zone, because I'd been told it was a very good school. So I gave the address of a close friend and luckily for me, the school accepted it. There was a bit involved in giving a fake address. I had to 'move' to that address ... kind of. Anyway, by the time my kids started Year One, we really were living in the catchment area, and we were also friends with Felicity, now living only a couple of blocks away from her. Sometimes my boys would be invited for a play with Lola at her house. Other times, she would come to our place after school. Charlie was still a baby—actually a toddler—so he wasn't going to school yet. When Lola visited, Felicity would stop by to pick her up, generally before dinner time. Sometimes we'd have drinks, sometimes we'd have tea, sometimes they'd all stay for dinner, and once, on a Friday, they all stayed for the night. Felicity and I had a few drinks, and we kissed—more than kissed, actually. She fell asleep next to me. I remember waking up in the middle of the night and seeing her face so close to mine. I gently kissed her chin, closed my eyes and fell asleep again. When I finally woke up, I was by myself. It was quite early, so I thought she might be in the kitchen making some tea or something. I sat up and noticed there was a note under my phone. I read *'Good morning. I am going for a walk. See you later. x'*

I thought that was strange since she wasn't the kind of person who goes for walks, especially early in the morning, but I simply shrugged, made myself some coffee and went back to bed for a bit. When she came back, she had been home and got changed. As she greeted me, I sensed a degree of detachment.

'You left so early. I thought you'd be coming back to have breakfast here.'

'Sorry, I just woke up and felt a bit restless. I didn't want to wake you, so I went for a walk, then I was so close to home that I thought I'd go in and shower.' She smiled at me, looked away, asked her children to help tidy up the twins' room, and said they were going home soon. I took advantage of the fact we were alone for a few minutes.

'Is something wrong?'

'What?' she said in an unconvincingly surprised tone.

'I just feel you're acting a bit odd.'

'No, I think I'm just tired.'

'Look, if this is about last night,'

She interrupted me. 'I really have to go. Sorry. We can talk later. Is that okay?'

I was silent for a moment before I could reply. I was staring at her, but she avoided my gaze.

'Okay.'

Right then, the kids came from the bedroom area, running across the living room into the kitchen. Our guests left shortly after.

Felicity kept avoiding me during the week. When I picked the kids up at school on Monday, she'd sent her sister to pick Lola up. I texted her and asked if she was okay but received no answer until the following morning.

'Hi, soz bout late reply. Had a migraine, better now. I hope you're well.'

I did not see her that day either, then on Wednesday, I saw her at drop-off time. I rang a few times throughout the week, but she never answered, nor did she return my calls. I decided to give her space and stopped messaging her altogether, although it was hard, and I was hurting. At the end of the second week, on a Friday morning, I received a text message: 'I miss you. When can I see you?'

I wanted to say, 'I miss you too. How about now?' but instead, I wrote, 'Hi. How are you? I'm working from home today. Can have a break at 11 if that suits.'

She arrived right at 11. We sat in the living room and started with some small talk.

'How have you been? Is the migraine fully gone?'

'Oh, that? Yes, It's gone.'

'That's good.'

'How about you?'

'Me? Well, I suppose I'm okay. I've been feeling like you were giving me the cold shoulder, and my attempts to call you and ask what was going on didn't work. You kept pushing me away, so I gave up.'

'Gave up?'

'Yes.'

'On what exactly?'

I shrugged.

'Did you give up on us?'

'I don't know, Felicity. I just got tired, okay? What did you expect? Did you want me to keep acting like a lost puppy, begging for your attention? For how long?'

She got closer to me, sighed deeply and grabbed my right hand with both of hers. Then she spoke while looking me in the eye. 'I'm so sorry. I've been feeling very distraught, and I've missed you. I've missed you terribly.'

'If you really have, how come you didn't return any of my calls?'

'Because I was nervous and scared. I don't know exactly of what, Clarissa. I've been asking myself that question, and I don't have an answer. I just know for sure I missed you, and I don't want to be away from you.'

'All right, I'm pretty sure this is about that night, I mean, the extra intimacy we shared. Felicity, what happened between you and I two weeks ago was as surprising for me. I'm saying this because I hope you don't think I'd planned it or something. That never happened. But truth be told, I don't regret it. If you do, and if you'd rather just be friends, that's fine. I'm okay with that. We're grown-ups, so let's just be open and honest.'

No sooner had I finished my last word than she started to speak. 'I think I'm in love with you.'

'What did you just say?'

She did not repeat but kissed me. It was short. Then we hugged. She was holding me very tight when I noticed she was crying.

'What's wrong?'

She didn't reply, so I continued. 'Do you wanna talk?'

'I don't know what to say.'

I waited a few seconds then asked, 'What do you need from me, right now?'

'Just be here with me.'

'Okay. I'm here. And I'm not going anywhere. All right?'

She nodded.

We stayed like that for a while. Eventually, she managed to speak a bit more and told me that she did not know what it meant to be in a gay relationship. 'What is it going to look like? In the future? How am I going to explain it to the kids? And to my folks?'

'Hey! We don't have to make any of those decisions now. Relax, okay? *You're* the one who generally gives me this kind of advice. Just breathe. We'll see how this unfolds.'

That night, she and her kids ended up staying at my place. When she and I were in my bedroom, ready to go to bed, she kissed me and started unbuttoning my shirt. I stopped her.

'I don't think we should do that.'

'Why not?'

'Because.'

'Because?'

'How about we take some time? We acted very impulsively last time. It ended up being too much for you. I don't want to cause another spiritual hangover.'

'You won't. I know that I want you.'

'Okay, but can we wait? I'll be anxious otherwise. We can still cuddle and kiss, but not more than that tonight.

'Sure. But, until when?'

'Until I'm sure that you are sure.'

'And how is that going to happen?'

'Well, to start with, if I wake up tomorrow and find a note saying you went for a walk, that's not going to help.'

She smiled and hugged me.

Our relationship grew steadily and smoothly. We spent a lot of our free time together, most of which included the kids, but we managed to do things on our own too, as it wasn't that hard to find someone to look after them for a night. Our dates were generally to restaurants or the movies. She wasn't comfortable with people knowing about her sexuality, so when we were out in public, we behaved like friends only. I was okay with that for a while, but as time went on, I started to feel tired, especially because her expectations were that I did not tell my own friends either, except for the ones who did not live in Australia.

It's 2021, and there's still discrimination. She wanted us to hide because she couldn't cope with the possibility of lack of acceptance. Meanwhile, I could not cope with living in the closet and hiding my true identity. That felt suffocating, degrading, soul-crushing. We'd been living this 'forbidden love' for over eighteen months, and she still wasn't sure about going public. To anyone.

Today most of my friends know, although my soul still feels crushed, and I still feel I'm suffocating, for other reasons, on and off. At least I don't feel I'm corrupting myself.

I recall the first time we had a lengthy conversation about coming out.

'Why is it so important to you that people know about our private life?'

'That is NOT true. The real question here is: Why do you feel it's so important to hide?'

'Because that's how we survive; that's how we dodge the reckless attacks of narrow-minded people.'

'You may not realise, but you're the one acting narrow-minded. Do you laugh with them when your narrow-minded colleagues make offensive jokes?'

'Of course not! How could you think that? And they're not like that. They don't make gay jokes.'

'So what is the big deal then? What are you scared of?'

'I just fear ... mostly for the kids.'

'I don't like living like a chameleon. I can never see your true colours in the wild. I only get to see you in intimacy. I'm tired! And also, that means I can't show my true colours either ... I'm becoming a liar ... a really good one, which is a bit scary. I don't want to model that to my kids.'

'We're just different, okay? What you want is too much. I'm not going to have my life displayed like I'm some celebrity, with photos of my private life on social media.'

'That's not what I want either. You are exaggerating here. I just want to be able to hold your hand when we are in the company of close friends, for instance, or with family. I can't cope with all this secrecy. I can't tell anyone I am in a relationship because if I do, you feel I'm betraying your trust. I feel you're embarrassed about being with me. Meanwhile, I'm so proud of you, of us, and I want to show you off to the people I care about; I want them to know I've found my soulmate. I want them to stop trying to find me a match.'

'You really have NO idea, do you?'

'Maybe if you tell me, I will.'

'You think it's uncomfortable that your friends try to find you a match? I tell you what: my dad has only finally stopped trying to force me to get back together with Phillip. I had to put up with that for years. Years of interference. If he realises I am in a relationship with a woman, I can't even imagine his reaction.'

'You are thirty-six years old. Explain to me why your father's reaction is more important than your freedom. I really would like to understand that. And also, what has that got to do with the kids?'

'The kids?'

'Yes. You said you fear for the kids.'

'There are things you don't know.'

'How about you tell me? I really would like to understand.'

'My mum isn't very stable. After my brother's tragedy, she was never the same.'

'Wait, what?'

CHAPTER 3

FELIX

So this is when I found out that Felicity had a brother. Had. Past tense. His name was Felix, and he was older than Felicity. When he was 16, Mark, their father, caught him making out with another boy, Connor, who was a year younger and happened to be from their church. It actually happened in the church, and both of them were disciplined. That meant they were not allowed to sing in the choir for the rest of the semester, and were excluded from the Easter play, for which they had both auditioned and had been given prominent roles.

This only gave them more free time. It was true they were not able to see each other at any of the rehearsals, but they kept meeting secretly, outside of the church. Their parents eventually found out. Mark became quite hostile towards Felix and eventually decided to send him to a private boarding school in a different state, even though it was the middle of the school year. Meanwhile, Connor's family had plans of their own to send him to study in Tasmania, where they had relatives.

The two of them wrote letters to each other—both unaware that Connor's family intercepted the letters. Despite that, they stayed in touch regularly, while their respective families hoped their affection for one another would simply die down as time passed.

The boys met again in the following summer holidays when they both returned to Perth to be with their family. They found ways to meet most days secretly. Felicity was an accessory, making sure she kept her parents out of the way so that Connor could get in and out of the house without being noticed. On one particular occasion, when Felicity was out, they were found in Felix's room. That really enraged Mark.

'I told you not to bring any visitors. My house, my rules.'

Felix left the house with Connor and walked with his friend to his house. When they were in front of it, they heard the creak of the front door opening and saw a tall and bulky human figure walk out. It was Anthony, Connor's dad. Connor turned to Felix and said goodbye before turning on his heels, opening the small wooden gate and stepping into the garden.

Felix raised his hand and bowed towards Connor's dad, who was standing still at the threshold, hands on hips. He did not acknowledge Felix back. Instead, he looked at his son and spoke. 'You think because you now have hair in your armpits you can do whatever you want? You cannot. And you still need to show respect.'

Felix saw the buckle loosen, the belt slide through each of the trousers' loops, go up into the air lifted by a large and fat hand, then fall heavily on Connor's back, once, twice, three times. Each time the leather met Connor's body, Felix heard a groan and noticed Connor curve his back. Felix asked him to stop, but the older man ignored him. So Felix walked through the gate and flung himself onto Anthony, who lost his balance, falling on his back. The two of them wrestled for a few seconds while Connor yelled at his dad, asking him to let Felix go. As his dad ignored his request, Connor grabbed hold of the hose, turned on the tap and aimed at them, mostly at his dad's head. Anthony got up while Connor went to Felix's assistance.

As Anthony stood up, he yelled, 'Get out of my house. And stay away from my son. I don't ever want to see you here again.'

Felix turned around and walked towards Connor's dad. Connor spoke, 'Just go, Felix, please,' and grabbed Felix by the arm, trying to pull him away. Felix kept walking in the opposite direction until he was very close to Anthony.

'The only person that should stay away from Connor is you, Sir. For his own safety. And I won't think twice about telling the police if I believe he's not safe.'

'Mind your own business or you'll find the police more likely to visit your place.'

'I'm shaking,' he said while still eyeballing Anthony.

Felix walked back home. His mother was about to serve dinner, not expecting her son to be home in time for the meal. Everyone looked at him in shock when they saw his state, water still dripping from his clothes.

Felicity was the first to speak. 'What happened?'

Felix didn't answer. He shuffled away noisily across the living room, and after he'd reached his bedroom, slammed the door closed. Felicity jumped to her feet and went to see him. She entered without knocking, then carefully closed the door again and stood staring at her brother. Before she was able to say anything, she noticed he was shaking. She saw Felix grab a large, thick rectangular cushion that was part of a small couch in his bedroom. It was very firm and solid. He propped it up on the sofa and started punching it.

'Felix, what is going on?'

Instead of replying, he went on throwing punches, which were accompanied by a groaning sound. Felicity waited for a couple of minutes, hoping Felix would wear himself out. As he continued to hit the cushion, she walked towards the couch, sat on it and slowly slid her arms behind the cushion, gently grabbing hold of it and shifting it closer to her until her upper body was behind it. Felix had to adjust his position. Felicity stayed as still as she could, holding the 'punchbag', until Felix collapsed onto his knees and leaned against the cushion, throwing both arms around it. He started roaring. Felicity moved away from behind the cushion but remained on the couch. She then stretched her arms towards Felix, in an invitation to embrace, which he accepted. He looked up at her. She could see his eyes welling up. He swallowed then managed to speak.

'Connor's not safe. He's not safe at home. I need to protect him.'

'What do you mean? Why is he not safe?'

'His dad. He belted him. Only stopped because I stopped him. I had to. But now I'm scared of what he might do to him tonight.'

Felix told Felicity everything that had happened. She decided to stay with him in his room for the rest of the night. They slept next to one another. When she woke up in the morning, Felix was doing push-ups on the floor. He started a strict exercising routine, which involved rope-skipping, sit-ups, and weightlifting, on top of the push-ups.

Chapter 4

Barefoot Walk

Another year started. Both Felix and Connor were in their last year at school, still a state away from each other. Connor's parents planned to send him to a university in England, as they thought anywhere else in Australia would not be far enough from Felix, who had no concrete plans for further education. Even before the two boys were caught kissing, Connor's family had plans for their son, who was a year ahead academically, having been accelerated back in primary school.

The two boys kept in touch, mainly through letters, but they also made phone calls to each other, both being boarders. They didn't meet again until July. Connor spent most school holidays with his family, whereas Felix only visited Perth for some of the breaks. The winter holiday was an important one because it was when they usually celebrated both his and Felicity's birthday, since the actual dates were in the end of June but the holidays generally started in July.

Felicity went to the airport with her parents to meet Felix. At first, she did not recognise him: he had a curtain haircut and had grown a goatee. He had also grown a bit and was looking stronger, with particularly toned arms. When she finally realised her brother was in front of her, she threw herself on him passionately! Felix didn't hug anyone else. Not even their mum. Biancha, their sister, was away at a friend's beach house and thus had not joined the family to the airport.

No sooner had they arrived home than Felix asked Felicity to go for a walk. The two of them walked barefoot through the streets of Shenton Park. Felix asked Felicity about her life, school, and church. She told him she'd started taking up drawing. He listened attentively while he took a pack of cigarettes from his pocket, put one cigarette between his lips and lit it.

'You're smoking?'

'Yes, Miss.'

'Since when?'

'A few months.'

'Can I try?'

'Hell, no!'

'Why not?'

'Because you're too young.'

Felicity didn't insist.

'Have you seen Connor?'

'Yes. He arrived last week and was in church. I noticed him looking around and thought he was searching for you. Are you planning to see him?'

'Definitely. Duh'

'What about his dad?'

'No, I'm not planning to see his dad.'

They both laughed.

'I was thinking that maybe you want to ask me something.'

'About what?'

'About Connor and I.'

'I don't. I just wish you still lived here. I miss you a lot. But I don't think It's bad or wrong that you're in love with Connor.'

'You don't?'

'It's very hard to think that way once you've watched *Fame.*'

'You've seen *Fame*? That's a bit advanced for your age.'

'Can you stop treating me like I'm a baby? I'm 13.'

'Okay, okay. You're right. I just worry about you. Specially now that I'm not around to look after you.'

Felix put his left arm around Felicity, and they kept walking together.

CHAPTER 5

GRIEF

Connor didn't look much different and didn't seem to mind Felix's new look either. Once he found out Felix was in town, they met most early mornings before sunrise. They'd go for a run together, then sit by the Jualbup Lake (which Felicity tells me was known as Shenton Park Lake back then) and chat. On Felix's last day in Perth, they exchanged jerseys, a kind of ritual they had started the previous time they'd met when they had exchanged t-shirts. That time, the weather wasn't appropriate for anything long-sleeved.

They planned to run away together next summer holidays, but Connor's father, who knew about the letters and the plans, kept Connor away for longer, so when Felix arrived home in December, there was no sign of Connor, and nobody seemed to know anything about him. His whole family was away.

That was as much as Felicity told me before I asked more questions.

'So what happened then?'

'Felix killed himself.'

'What? Why?' I asked in shock. Felicity was tearful but managed to keep speaking.

'I don't know,' she said, shaking her head then wiping her tears.

I got up to grab the packet of tissues and passed one to her.

'What do you mean, you don't know? I'm sorry, this is probably really hard for you, but I'm trying to understand.'

I paused for a short moment, then went on.

'It's not quite adding up. Wouldn't he have waited for Connor to return?'

'Maybe Felix saw no end. Maybe he felt there was no way out. Maybe he believed the rubbish he was told in church. I don't know... I don't know either.'

She started to weep intensely. My head was spinning, and I had a myriad of questions but decided it was best to remain silent. I cuddled her, and for a while she stayed still with her head resting on my left shoulder, her mouth just under my chin. All I managed to say was, 'I'm so sorry, my darling.'

She went on speaking. 'I should have been with him. We were going to make a gingerbread house, but I was waiting to be picked up from my scouts' club, and no one came.

'Then one of the leaders told me my dad's car had broken down and that I was going to stay at the club for a bit longer, but that I should not worry. I told her I could walk home, that I knew the way, but she didn't let me go.'

She repeated that last phrase a few times between sobs.

After that conversation, Felicity avoided me again for a few days, but she sent me short messages of reassurance. Then she came over for breakfast one morning, but I felt she was slightly detached, and she did not stay over any night at the weekend. She told me she was working on a new project that was keeping her very busy. I figured she needed some alone time, and much as I missed her, I needed some of that too.

It took a while until I found the right moment to talk to her about her family. Mainly, I wanted to understand a bit more about the dynamics.

'So you were three children in total? Felix, Biancha, and you?'

'Yes, that's right'.

'Did you ever feel your parents had a favourite?'

'Not really. Dad was very critical of Felix, but I guess it was because he was the eldest. And the only male child. I was still a kid when he left us, although I thought I was so grownup.'

'Is it upsetting for you to talk about this?'

'I can handle it,' she said and smiled at me.

You told me that your mum was never herself again after your brother passed. I can obviously understand why but … what happened to her?'

'At first, she was inconsolable. Out of control. Cried for days, didn't want any food, didn't want to talk to anyone, broke some stuff randomly, like plates and vases, and yelled a lot. She moved into Felix's bedroom and wouldn't let Dad get near her. Whenever he tried, she'd say something like, "Get away from me. You killed my son." Then with time she calmed down, but she wasn't the same as before. She was aloof most of the time but often angry towards Dad. She got lost once.'

'How come?'

'She left the house and didn't come back. We were all worried. The police brought her back. Said she was found alone wandering, unsure of who she was.'

'Who looked after you and Biancha?'

'I don't know. We were all in shock and grieving. Dad did what he could.'

'Did you have any contact with Connor after that?'

'No. Biancha did. She said that once Connor told her it was his fault. He believed that Felix assumed that he, Connor, did not want to run away with him, and that this had been why Connor did not come to Perth to meet Felix at the time they agreed.

'He told Biancha that he found out that his father, Anthony, had read the letters and made sure Connor was away for the date Connor and Felix had agreed to go away together.'

'Have you ever spoken to your parents about it?'

'I tried a few times. Dad always refused to answer any questions, so I gave up.' She paused for a moment, then got up and said, 'I think I need a cigarette. Can we go outside?'

We stayed in the courtyard for perhaps half an hour, mostly talking about our plans for the weekend. I asked her if she wanted me to invite her parents over for dinner, so they could get to know me better.

Fli told me about a difficult conversation when she had dinner with them recently. She told me how her dad had asked her when she was going to introduce them—meaning him and Ophelia—to a man, as in a potential partner. She replied with another question, asking what if she introduced them to a lady. Mark told her not to be ridiculous, and she said, 'What would you do? Can't send me away like you did with Felix.' He hit the roof and told her she was drunk and that he would drive her home. She replied she did not need a cab and that she wanted to talk about Felix.

'I want to know what happened to my brother.'

'You already know what happened to him: he made some very poor choices, against everything he'd learned about God, and he died.'

'Well, I think it was YOU who made a bad choice in sending him away!'

The conversation got nowhere. Felicity would not back off. Mark insisted on driving her home, and she repeated she did not need a lift.

She told me that during the shouting match with Mark her mum had covered her ears, and started repeating the words, 'My boy, my boy', and then she started crying. Following that, she started reciting some verses from the Bible.

'Blessed are those who hunger and thirst for righteousness, for they shall be satisfied.'

(Matthew 5:6)

Felicity said that Ophelia kept saying that over and over. She told me she looked it up straight away on her phone and saw it was from the Book of Matthew. She made a note, as she didn't want to forget.

'So my point is, they aren't ready. Not yet. And seeing Mum like that, I don't think I'm ready either.'

'Okay. I understand.'

CHAPTER 6

A PLAN THAT BACKFIRED

I actually did not mean for her to invite her parents to make an announcement. It was just so that they would get to know me better. I thought if we started trying to socialise a bit more, maybe it would help Felicity relax a bit more. But it wasn't meant to happen yet. That was in 2016. Although I did meet her family eventually, as a friend of hers, Felicity did not seem any more relaxed.

The year 2017 was special. Maybe it had to do with the referendum and the 'Yes Day'. Felicity and I never spoke about marriage, and I don't think this was on her mind or mine, but legalising marriage was important to us because it was part of our fight for equal rights, the right to love. So, I saw Felicity become a bit more involved and active in voicing her opinion. I thought with that would come the courage to come out, but that didn't happen that year either. Finally, in 2018, she said she was going to do it. I suggested telling a close friend first, someone from the same generation, then maybe she'd gain confidence after a while. She said she didn't trust anyone enough.

'Not even your best friend?'

'Honey, YOU are my best friend!'

She paused, as if waiting for me to say something. As I didn't, she continued:

'It's not that I don't trust my friends, like I think they'll intentionally betray me. I just think that they may not be able to contain themselves, and they'll talk about it, and then more people will know, so it may become garbled as it goes through the rumour mill. I'd rather be the one telling people.'

She insisted she wanted to start with her family, while I personally thought that was the hardest way.

She rehearsed a few times and chose different occasions to tell them. First Easter, but then she thought it would be a sacrilege to them. After that, she tried to tell them one Sunday, as we'd been invited to a Christmas-in-July lunch at their house, but Australia had lost a match during the world cup and was sent back home. Since Felicity's dad was very upset, she thought it wasn't the best time either. There was always a problem, always a 'but'.

'Perhaps you can just invite them to your place and say there's something you'd like to discuss.'

'I can't do that. Not like that.'

'Why not?'

'I don't know how to explain it, but I'd prefer it to be a special occasion, so they can't get out of it.'

'What d'you mean?'

'My parents, especially my dad, are very good at avoiding uncomfortable situations. If he's alone with me and he isn't comfortable, he'll just get up and leave, but if there are others around, then he'll stay to save face.'

'So you're saying that you would prefer to embarrass him in front of other people?'

'Whose side are you on? And It's not about embarrassing. It's more like having at least one witness.'

'Okay. So how about you invite them for dinner and then you invite me too?'

'He can still make up an excuse and not come. But if there's already a reason to meet, then he'll have no choice.'

I didn't agree with her reasoning but thought it was her choice, so I dropped the subject.

She tried again at Halloween, but her mum got sick. The next obvious choice was Christmas, but that was the worst possible option, as Felix had died around Christmas time.

Finally, in 2019, for her birthday, we had planned to 'come out' as an item, announce it to the world. Just like before, she intended to tell her parents first. She told me it was only easy for me because my parents did not live here.

And maybe she's right. I will probably never know. My mum has never liked the idea of me being with a woman, but it is what it is.

This new plan of telling her parents about our relationship at her birthday celebration started in about March, when we started planning her party. I tried to persuade her to perhaps do it just herself, her sister for support, and the parents, as I claimed they may feel uncomfortable with me at first.

'No, I'll need you there.'

'They may have questions for you, but if I'm there, they may not feel they can ask.'

'You don't know them. If you're not there, they'll run over me and then most likely act like nothing happened and that I never told them anything. They are very good at avoiding and dismissing.'

'Sweetheart, it is your choice when to tell them, what to tell them, and how. It is NOT your choice how they react.'

'What are you saying?'

'I'm saying that perhaps it's better not to have expectations about their reaction and try to focus on the message you want to deliver. Because you can control what you say, but you can't control how people receive it.'

'I think you're right. Thanks.'

So the night came. I picked her up from her house in a cab, and we went to a special venue in the Swan Valley. I'd made a booking for seven people, as we'd invited her parents, her sister, and two of her closest friends, one of them from work. Most of them were quite late, but her sister was already there when we arrived. We ended up being eight, but that was a surprise.

Her sister, Biancha, was waiting outside. At the entry, an usher gave us an envelope that contained 10 character cards. It was an Ancient Greek theme night, and guests had to pick a card to determine who they were. Biancha got Athena, Felicity got Helen, and I got Odysseus. We were then directed to a kind of a cloakroom, where we exchanged our card for a costume. This was all included in the price. Actually, we had to pay a deposit, which would be fully refunded once we returned the outfits. Each outfit had a tag with its equivalent character name, so people were easily identified.

Felicity was extremely nervous, as this was 'The Day'. We ordered drinks, and she started to relax more, or so I thought. When her two other friends arrived, she became very talkative and assertive, but her assertiveness seemed directed at me only.

At one point, I was invited to sing a song with the band. That had been arranged by me, as I was friends with the bass player. As I stood in front of the microphone, I said, 'Good evening, everyone. My name's Clarissa Torres, and I'd like to sing a song to a very special lady. You know who you are. Happy birthday!' So I sang *True Colors* by Cindy Lauper.

The crowd seemed to like it, and they sang along when we got to the chorus. When I finished the song, I thanked the band, the audience, and I went back to our table. Her parents had arrived. I greeted them and was informed they had brought along someone called Tom, who seemed over-friendly with Felicity. I had to try to find an empty chair and drag it to our table as Tom had taken my seat. I ended up sitting next to him.

'Hi. I'm Tom. You're the neighbour, right?'

'Pardon?'

'They told me while you were singing. I used to be her neighbour too when we were in high school.'

'Oh, so you're the ex then,' I said smiling. He looked puzzled.

'What?'

'You're the ex-neighbour. And I'm the current one.'

'Right.'

He turned his head to look at her, and they both laughed. Then Tom stretched his hand to shake mine. I wanted to crush it, but I'm not that strong.

He said, 'It's really nice to meet you, Clarissa.'

'Actually, tonight I'm Odysseus. Who are you tonight?'

Felicity laughed and licked her upper lip, something I noticed she did when she was nervous. She grabbed the envelope and asked Tom to pick a card. He looked at the three last cards: one was Paris, one was Elpenor, and one was Patroclus.

'Well, I'd love to be Paris for the night if I get to steal you, Helen!'

Everyone laughed but me. I said, 'Watch your back. Agamemnon could be lurking somewhere.' But my comment was followed by blank faces, so I just took a large sip of my drink.

Felicity's parents made a nice comment about my singing. The word 'neighbour' kept echoing inside my head. Fli kept avoiding my gaze, and her sister tried to make polite conversation. Tom excused himself to go to the restroom. As he stood up, he asked if anyone wanted another drink. We all declined, and when he returned, now as Paris, he had a margarita for him and one for Fli.

'A special drink for the birthday girl.'

'Well, thank you!'

At eight o'clock, everyone went into the huge dance floor, and instead of a band, there was an event leader, giving us instructions. Each person had to find their match. Odysseus had to find Penelope, Achilles had to find either Briseis or Patroclus, and so on and so forth. However, the rule was that you could not simply go and find your match. Each person had the name of the possible matches on the reverse of their tag, which also showed whether they belonged to Sparta or Troy.

All participants started dancing with anyone and had to change dancing partner every time the song stopped until they got their match. The trick was that some characters had a secret weapon. This weapon could only be used against a character that, according to the legend, had been killed by that particular character. For example, Hector could kill Patroclus, and Achilles could kill Hector, whereas only dear Paris could kill Achilles. I felt really angry that I did not have Agamemnon's card.

Another twist was that some people had monster characters, like the Cyclops and Medusa. Those characters could kill anyone. Then some people had a god or goddess. These were allowed to pick whoever they wanted for a match.

The dance floor was divided into three parts, two parallel cordon-like ropes acting like the boundary lines. The section at one end was called Sparta. The middle section was a common ground, where all participants started looking for their match. It was also where the dead ones stayed. The other side was Troy.

If a person requested to dance with someone who was already matched, they were sent to whichever dance floor they did not belong to as a slave. For instance, if Paris was with Helen, and a third character requested to dance with either of them, that person was the one who'd become a slave, unless they were a monster or a god. Only monsters and gods could split a matched couple. It was a cool game, and I did my best to enjoy it, even if simply for the sake of a tribute to Homer, whom I admire as a writer.

I found my Penelope quite early, and I thought I'd stay with her for the rest of the game, but Athena, who was Biancha, intervened and separated us. I spent almost the rest of the night with her, even after the game ended.

Felicity's parents went home after the game, and the rest of us stayed on the dance floor. At some point, they started playing a mixture of some slow dance music and some old dance music, and I saw how Paris was enjoying his cheek-to-cheek moment with Helen. Biancha, still as Athena, saw it too and looked at me, disconcerted. Then she spoke.

'She's had a bit to drink.'

'Sounds like that's what I should do too. Want some?'

'Dance this song with me. Then we'll get a drink.'

'Sure!'

I already suspected that Biancha knew about Felicity and me. At that moment, I felt certain. I held her right hand with my left and danced what was left of *Great Pretender* and the beginning of *Be My Baby*. Biancha tried to cheer me up as if she could fix things, just like gods do. She cleverly manoeuvred us towards Felicity and Tom, then she separated their hands, and somehow the four of us were holding hands in a line. Biancha placed herself right in front of Tom. 'I deserve some of your attention too!' And they slowly—too slowly for my liking—moved further from Felicity and me.

I was unsure whether I was Odysseus or Clarissa. I was unsure if I was awake or dreaming. I was unsure if Felicity was my girlfriend or my ex. She was in front of me. Happiness was escaping me. We remained holding hands, and the song *Classic* by Adrian Gurvitz started. I was looking right into her eyes. She looked tipsy but cheerful.

'I'm just teasing him. You know I don't like him, right?'

'Are you sure It's not me you're teasing?'

'C'mon!'

'I thought tonight was about the truth, not teasing anyone.'

'Well, tonight's about me!'

'And who are you, by the way? I can't recognise you.'

'Look, I know we had an agreement, and you have expectations. But ... do you have any idea of how awkward it would be to do it tonight? I mean, Tom wasn't even invited, but my parents brought him, and he's probably thinking we're still in high school.'

'Then wake him up from his dream and show him this isn't high school.'

'It would be awkward for him. Put himself in his place.'

'Don't you mean put *myself* in his place? Anyway, I don't really care about him, to be honest. The question is, can you put yourself in my place?'

In a fit of anger, she pulled away, but somehow her necklace got caught in my dress, and as she moved, the necklace broke. The pendant, which was a pair of gold wings I'd given her the year before, fell off. The necklace was still attached to my clothes, in front of my bosom. As she snatched the chain, it ripped part of my toga.

She left impetuously. I picked up my wings, which had been abandoned by their guardian but returned to their owner.

I went into the restroom, and it was only when I was in front of the mirror that I noticed how bad the damage to the toga was. That meant I would not be able to return it and get my refund. I thought of my best friend, Dominique, and her business. I wished I was home so I could ring her.

First Aid Seamstress, good morning. Triage, intensive care, IVF or transplant unit?

Dominique runs a mobile sewing business. Very successful. She has a few people working for her at different shifts. Her busiest days are weekends when most people dress up and go out. So I thought if anyone could help me at that moment, it had to be her. No one else.

I came back from the restroom. Felicity was by the bar, so I joined her. Somehow Biancha was still dancing with Tom, but the song stopped and I noticed he turned around as if looking for someone. He spotted Felicity and started walking towards us. Another romantic song had just started. Biancha was following Tom. As he was about to reach Felicity, Biancha pulled him towards herself, placed her hand behind his neck and kissed him. I saw how, after a few seconds, he pulled away from her. He turned his head slightly and looked at Felicity, then me.

I smiled and joked, 'Come on, Paris. You can't contradict a goddess.'

So he obeyed.

Making an effort not to ruin her special day, I allowed my night to be ruined. Biancha had driven and offered to give us a lift, but Felicity said she wasn't ready to go yet. Tom jumped at the opportunity to stay alone with Felicity.

'I can stay with Felicity. I'll look after her.'

'Are you sure you want to stay, Felicity?' I asked.

'Yes, I'm getting old, but the night's young.'

'Okay, I'm going. Take care.'

I didn't even bother to say goodbye properly to Tom. I walked towards the exit door, while Biancha stayed behind for a couple of minutes. As I reached the exit, I turned around one last time, hoping to find that Felicity had changed her mind and decided to come home. I saw Biancha walking towards me, and far away near the bar, I saw Tom hold Felicity's hand, smile at her, and get a smile back. I felt like there was a hand inside my chest and the hand grabbed my heart and squeezed it so tight that I gasped for air.

We were directed to the cloakroom again, where we got changed into our own clothes and walked to the car park.

Biancha and I were quiet for a good part of the ride. The radio was on, which helped make the silence less awkward. She stopped the car in front of my place and turned the ignition off. I thanked her for driving me home and asked if she wanted a cup of tea.

'No, I don't want to trouble you. You should just rest. But if you think you need company, I'll come inside with you for a bit.'

'I'll be okay. My au pair's inside.' Then I broke down.

'Hey!' She hugged me and sighed, 'This is a very awkward situation, and appalling behaviour, most unlike my sister. I'm feeling embarrassed about her. I'm really sorry.'

'May I ask a question? Were they … like an item, like really official, kind of thing? Back then? Or was it just a teenage thing?'

'D'you wanna know if they slept together back then? No, they didn't. But I'll tell you what: if he shags as poorly as he kisses, he'll be single for a long time!'

I laughed. 'Was it that bad?'

'Oh my Lord! I need to erase that memory.'

'Why did you kiss him?'

'I was trying to steer him away from you and Fli. I just pretended I had spotted an ex of mine and told Tom I wanted to act like he and I were together, just while "my ex" was looking at me. But hey, enough about him. Thanks for the night, for organising everything, and also for singing that beautiful song. And I'm really sorry.'

I shook my head and swallowed. 'It's not your fault.' I wiped the tears off my face with both hands, smiled, thanked her again for the lift and said goodnight.

The four children were asleep, and my au pair was by herself, sitting on the rug, her back against the couch. I felt slightly comforted by seeing her. I remember when I received the form from the au pair agency. When I read her application and found out her name was Dominique, an involuntary smile invaded me. That's how I chose her, on pure intuition. I call her 'Domi' to make the distinction.

When she noticed me walk into the house, she was surprised.

'I thought you were staying at Felicity's.'

'Yeah, me too, but she wanted to keep partying, and I wasn't feeling great.'

'Oh no! I'm really sorry to hear that.'

'It's okay. It's nice to be home early and the kids asleep. It gives me a chance to go to bed and read, or stay on the couch, or whatever I want,' I lied.

'Would you like me to make you a tea?'

'I'd love a tea.'

Domi made a pot of tea, and we both sat on the rug and chatted for quite a while. She told me more about her plans to travel around the country, how she wanted to live on a farm for a while, then return to her home country and be a farm vet. She also told me about her ex-boyfriend, how she'd broken up with him and how much her family criticised her for doing so, and that she still felt guilty about it but that she knew that deep inside, she did not love him.

I wasn't sure whether Domi knew about the nature of my relationship with Felicity, and I didn't really care one way or another. I'd have told her or let her figure out if Felicity hadn't gone out of her way to hide our relationship. Having said that, Domi was a smart girl, and as they say and I believe, women have a sixth sense, so she could have at least suspected.

As we drank our tea, Domi smiled and spoke, 'Can I read your palm?'

'I don't know. Can you?'

We both laughed, then I stretched my left hand out to her.

'Mmmm. Very interesting.'

'What?'

'I'm trying to interpret it. Do you want more children?'

'I don't think so. Why? Will I have more?'

'Well, this is like the potential. But the choice is always yours.'

'What about the father?'

'I can't see that … I can only see a potential person in your life, like a really important one. It doesn't mean It's the father.'

'Okay. What else can you see?'

'A change.'

'A change? Of what?'

'I'm not too sure,' she said, then laughed. 'You probably think I'm making this up.'

'No, I don't. C'mon. What else?'

'Well, it could be a career change … It's something significant, like breaking away from something major.'

'Can it be breaking away from someone?'

She looked at me in the eye, very earnestly. The back of my hand was resting on her left palm. Then, with her other hand, she started wrapping my hand with hers, gently folding my fingers so that in the end, my hand was shaped into a fist.

'Yes, it could be that. But It's a really big one.'

'Could it be someone's death?'

'No. That would appear differently. More like a loss. Although ...'

'Although?'

'I don't want to say it because I don't want you to be thinking about death; It's way too serious, and this little sign I saw here isn't enough. Can we have Turkish coffee? Then I'll read your cup. Just to compare.'

I agreed, and then a few minutes later, we were drinking black coffee with some sugar cubes. Once I finished, she told me to turn my cup upside down, over the saucer.

'You do it. I don't want to do it the wrong way.'

'No, no, no. You have to do it yourself. If I do it, then it doesn't work. And there's no wrong way. It's your way.'

'Okay. So ... Do I do it slowly? Fast?'

'Don't think about it. Just do it.'

I turned my cup and rested it on the saucer and stared at her beautiful, deep blue eyes.

'Now what?'

'Now we wait.'

'How long?'

'Just a bit. Let's chat.'

A few minutes passed and she asked me to pick my cup up. I turned it over and examined it carefully, then gave it to her. As she frowned, I asked, 'What can you see? Is it good?'

'Everything can be good or bad.'

She moved closer to me and started pointing to some patterns inside the cup.

'See the animal?'

'Nope. Which animal?'

'Here, look! Can you see? Four legs, a tail …'

'Oh yes! So, are you sure this isn't your cup? Like you know, you want to be a vet, right?'

We both laughed

'No, that's your cup.'

'So? What does it mean?'

'Well, what animal do you think it is? I don't want to influence you, but … if you look carefully, there are some signs there.'

'Like?'

'Well, you tell me.'

'Okay. Um … Well, the tail is quite prominent.'

'Unhum. And where is it pointing?'

'Up.'

'Exactly.'

'Oh my gosh. I think It's a cat.'

'That's my impression too. Do you like cats?'

Umm … I don't dislike them. I just, you know, prefer dogs. Like I've had cats, and I've been close to other people's cats too. Actually, there was only one cat that was really loyal to me. Unfortunately, I left her behind now that I think of it. I rescued her together with my housemate, that's like … 15 years ago, before I came to Australia.'

'Then what happened?'

'Well, I had to come here … and the cat stayed with my housemate.'

There was a pause. Then I continued. 'So, do you think that's my old cat?'

'Definitely not! Also, this isn't really about the past as much as it's about the present.'

'And future?'

Yes, future too. But often, it is the imminent present, but people don't see that certain things are already happening. They think about a new job as the future, but they have already deep inside decided to leave their current job … something like that. So in this case, the cup would be showing the present, and it's up to the person to take action and make that state become real, like put it in motion.'

'Interesting.'

'But let's go back to the cat.'

'Maybe I'll adopt a cat?'

'Well … look at this. What can you see next to the cat?'

'What's that? A ghost?'

We laughed.

'I see definitely something floating … Almost like wings, but it's like … the wrong angle.'

'Broken wings! I got it.'

'Really?'

'I think so.'

'So the cat and the wings are like aiming at opposite directions. If we look the way the wings are pointing to this side, can you see this part here?'

'Yes.'

'Can you see a human figure?'

'I can.'

'Can you see how this person has the arm sticking out?'

'I can, yes. Like they're pointing?'

'Maybe. But the arm is very low. The angle, I mean, it could be that they're just waiting for someone, offering a hand. Then there are some trees. See?'

'Yes.'

'So that's it.'

'And what does it mean?'

'When I read your palm, I saw a big change. Now with the cup, I'm thinking the wings represent your force. You can fly towards the cat, which has its head turned away from you, if you are the wings, or you can fly towards the forest. I think it's the safe and familiar versus the primitive and "unknown".'

'But why do you think the cat's safe? And why would a helping hand not be safe?'

'The cat is safe only because it's urban life, or family life, domestic life, like a similar routine. That's what I'm getting from it. The helping hand could be good or bad. It could be great, but so far, it's unknown. It could be you too.'

'Perhaps I can take the helping hand AND the cat.'

'Yeah, why not?! The possibility is there if you see it. Sometimes we are conditioned to choose when we see more than one option but often life gives us a multiple-choice question.'

'Wow, you're good! You sound so convincing. Did you study this?'

'No, I don't believe in studying this stuff. My grandmother used to read our cups most nights. I loved it. She used to start a story, like a bedtime story.'

'Really?'

'Yes.'

'She'd make up a story out of random figures in a dirty cup?'

'She wasn't making it up. She was reading it, and then, with her, I learned to read too.'

We stayed up a bit more, then I said goodnight and went to have a shower. Domi stayed in the living room and asked if she could watch a movie or whether the noise would bother me. I said she could watch whatever she wanted for as long as she wanted.

I went into my room and started to undress. Then I remembered I'd kept the wings in my bra, between my bra and my breast. I placed them on my palm and stared at them for a while. I closed my hand tight, holding the wings, scared they'd fall or fly away from me. Then I got my jewellery box out, extracted a gold chain from it, and threaded the chain through the pendant's loop. I put the chain on and went to have my shower. I shed a few tears under the water but somehow felt comforted by my wings.

I didn't hear from Felicity the following day, nor did I try to contact her. I had ordered a special breakfast for two, which was to be delivered to her house. I hope she enjoyed it. I hope she ate her share and mine. I hope she put on a couple of kilos. I got no acknowledgement whatsoever. At home, we had pancakes with maple syrup. I let the kids make it, although they left the kitchen in a state that is even hard to describe. We have a burgundy red feature wall in our kitchen, but it featured some off-white distorted-polka dots from when they used the mixer.

Charlie accidentally tore the bag of flour then in no time, I saw the four of them playing with it. I would normally put a stop to that straight away, but I was in no mood for rules, so I just scooped some of the flour and sprinkled it to my own hair. They all laughed and copied me. We ended up looking like ghosts, all very white. We ate the pancakes, and then I made all of them shower and get changed, and I did the same. Then I asked the four of them to tidy up the bedroom with me. They made the bed—or at least they think they did.

They picked up all the clothes that were on the floor and put them in the laundry basket, then they picked up some odd toys and put them in the drawers. Later, after lunch, I asked if Domi would take Charlie and Lola back home. She asked me no questions, and I was sure she had understood the situation. I gave her my car keys and told her I had no plans to go out and if she wanted to go somewhere, she could. It was Sunday, and it was raining, and all I wanted to do was stay home in my pyjamas.

Then the thought that Felicity may not have spent the night alone crossed my mind, and I felt very anxious. I told myself not to think about that, but it was too late. *Is this why she didn't even ring me? Is she feeling guilty? Or has she realised she's straight after all? Perhaps she doesn't know how to tell me that she doesn't want to be with me anymore.* It was rather tortuous. I tried to comfort myself with lines like, *I no longer care*, or *Don't be silly! Biancha said he can't even kiss properly*, but that wasn't enough to put my mind at ease.

Domi came back about an hour later. My twins got picked up by their father, as they'd be spending the first week of the winter holidays with him. With the kids gone, the house felt even colder. I turned on the music and decided to light the fire.

I noticed the day get darker through my side window. I noticed birds flying to the top of the trees, probably getting ready for the night. Then I thought of the wings in the coffee cup and the trees.

Domi said she'd cook for us, and I offered no objection to that.

We drank wine, ate and chatted some more. The inevitable question came.

'So what happened last night?'

I sighed.

'It's more like what didn't happen.'

'Okay. What was meant to happen?'

'My … girlfriend, who I believe is now my ex, was going to tell her family that we were in a relationship and that she identifies as gay.'

We both took a sip of our respective drinks.

'Did she get cold feet?'

I shrugged.

'We'd planned this. For a long, long time.'

Domi pulled the long sleeves of her grey pullover towards her hands until her fingers could not be seen. She nodded, encouraging me to continue.

'This weird guy who she knew from her school years came to her party, and he was like, all over her, salivating for her!'

'D'you think she likes him back?'

I didn't want to admit I was jealous and actually wondering whether something might have happened between them the night before, and what is worse, if they'd continue seeing each other.

'No! I don't know. I don't think so. I think she likes the idea of being straight … or being admired. I don't know. Or perhaps she thinks that's what her parents want.'

'How long have you … known her?'

'A few years. We've been together for about four.'

'Is she out to anyone?'

'Not really.'

'That's hard. Did you ever think about maybe some therapy? Couples' therapy?'

'I did, but she thought it would expose her, like, she'd be caught, officially.'

'Oh no! It's like … no way out. Was she at least pro-freedom? the words in English, but … what I mean is …'

'I know what you mean. Yes, she says she believes in equal rights and all that. And she voted for same-sex marriage, and we went to celebrate together for the "YES Day".'

'Yes Day? Did someone propose? Who was getting married?'

I chuckled, then explained. 'Oh, you weren't here yet. We had a referendum in 2017. People had to vote "yes" or "no" about whether they wanted to legalise same-sex marriage. And we won. It was great. The whole country celebrated.'

'So you were out together during that night?'

'Yes, we were. But we never held hands or anything. She'd never do that that in public.'

CHAPTER 7

UNHAPPY BIRTHDAY

J ust over a week later, it was my birthday. I was at work, in my room at the wellness centre, when they called me on the phone saying someone wanted to see me. I walked out of the room, went down the stairs and met this odd, eccentric stranger at the reception.

'Clarisse Torres?'

'Yes. But it's Clarissa.

'I was sent to deliver you this'—and she removed a bag that looked like a sack from her back, out of which she extracted a stringed musical instrument that looked a bit like a banjo and a bit like a uke. She started strumming and singing at the same time:

'Happy birthday is such an easy phrase,

Happy birthday should really be your fate,

Happy birthday and lots of yummy cake,

Happy birthday; I think I made a mistake.

Please forgive me for being so weak,

Without you, my future is bleak,

I just need time, patience, okay I'm a freak,

You're my bird and I miss your little beak.

Happy birthday you wished me on that night,

A special dinner you planned, and not a fight.

I still think our future can be bright,

If you wait 'til I feel a bit more light.

Would you like another dance?

Oh please give me one more chance.

I'm not fit to take a stance.

All I want is some romance.

Would you like another dance?

I will never be quite your height,

In strength, assertiveness, all right?

But hold my hand and I will delight,

Lie next to me, close your eyes, and turn off the light,

This is not fantastic, but neither is it plastic,

And I wrote it in the attic, thinking of you, last night.'

I'm not sure what she expected. I'm not sure what intention she had, but the truth is, I did not feel flattered. At all. In fact, on top of the embarrassment I felt for having this strange person that looked like a hippy from the 1970s call out my name at my workplace, I felt offended. 'All I want is some romance?' What is that supposed to mean? Go and romance handsome Tom, then!

When I got home, there was a bunch of flowers on my porch. Without even getting close to it, I walked inside, got changed and made my way out again. I picked the flowers up and walked towards the park. I found a restaurant, walked inside and searched the place quickly until I spotted a well-dressed man. I walked up to him and said, 'Hi. I know this will sound crazy, but you look like you're waiting for your date. Here are some flowers you can give to her. Or him.'

I left before he could say anything. Then I took my earphones from my pocket, connected them to my phone, put my music on and started jogging. I jogged, and I jogged, and I jogged until I could hardly breathe. It felt great. From that day, jogging became a drug to me, or medicine … is there a difference? The thing is, jogging helps. It's as if I run away from something, and it works…When I finish, I feel I'm really far away from wherever I was before.

CHAPTER 8

CUPID AND TATTOOS

I ran throughout winter and into spring. Now the warmest season had almost arrived. The magpies were very present, protecting their nests, and the trees I had seen completely bare now looked very leafy, making the park a verdant sight. As we slid through spring, its smell got progressively stronger, just like when you approach a busy kitchen but after you stay there long enough, your sense of smell adapts and gets momentarily desensitised. It felt like the more I ran, the closer I was to summer, the further from winter.

In November, Domi decided to leave town on a road trip. So I placed an ad on housemate.com because I wanted to see how I'd feel having a housemate instead of an au pair. A total of five girls came to see the house, and I chose someone called Leanne. She was slim, athletic, had short straight hair and somehow gave an air of assertiveness, especially in the way she walked. She was 33.

She only wanted to stay for the summer, as she intended to move to Ireland. She was a tattoo artist and also a painter. I told her I had always wanted to have a tattoo but had always felt scared. She showed me her three tattoos and encouraged me to get the one I wanted, but I did not want to share my idea with her, so I just pretended I didn't know what kind of tattoo I wanted, nor where.

Leanne painted two of our walls. She doesn't just paint walls like with conventional paint. She decorates them. So I told her I wanted the wall behind my bed to look like the ocean and the sky, blended together. I told her to feel free to add some features. She ended up drawing an ocean, a ship on the high seas, and Jupiter (the God, not the planet) looking down from the sky, as Venus, Mercury and Cupid, their son, sail to a land of mortals.

I asked her, 'What made you choose that?'

'I don't know. I had a look at your book collection to try to find out more about you. There was a lot about Judaism, but that gave me no inspiration. I was impressed by your collection of Freud's work but again, no inspiration there. Plus, my view is that he was a misogynist, so I wouldn't use him in my art. Not even if you paid me … And then there was your section of Greek and Roman mythology … The only other option apart from that was Harry Potter, and I thought this'd be more appropriate.'

She said all that looking very serious. I laughed. She remained impartial.

Some time in December, I finally got my tat. A set of wings. On my back. I wanted to go out and show everyone, but I had to keep out of the sun for quite a while—and it was summer. So I kept it out of sight for the whole month. Then one Saturday, Leanne, the kids and I went to the beach. She did not own any bathers. I offered to lend her some, but she said she didn't need bathers. She liked wearing her clothes, as in, her plain clothes. I asked her to wear at least the top part of one of my bikini sets. She took a look at them then, funnily enough, picked a hot pink piece that Felicity and I had bought together—we had a matching set. I had always been quite protective of that piece, but I am not sure I cared anymore. If I did, then I was trying hard not to. It was hard to tell. Leanne put it on then covered it with a singlet.

At the beach, as I took my t-shirt off, my kids spotted the tat.

'Mummy, you have a tattoo?'

'Yes, I do! D'you like it?'

They were fascinated. Leanne examined the work carefully and made a compliment. 'Very fine tracing and good use of colours.'

We spent about three hours at the beach. The boys tried to teach Leanne how to play "frescobol", better known as beach paddle ball, and she was not bad at it. We all went for a swim. The water was calm and not too cold. When I announced we had to go, the boys wanted to stay more, but

I'd had enough and Leanne was looking sunburned, so we made our way back home. Leanne offered to cook for us, and I made no effort to resist. While she prepared the food, I folded the washing and vacuumed. I then opened a bottle of white wine and offered her a glass. To my surprise, she said she didn't drink. I asked why not, and she said she simply had never been interested and that all her friends that drank had problems, so she thought there must be something wrong with drinking.

'Okay. Thanks. Now I know where my problems come from: the bottle,' I said, joking.

'I don't mean it like that.'

'How do you mean then?'

She shrugged. 'You know what? I'm curious now. I am going to have a glass.'

So I poured her a glass. After a couple of sips, it was evident she was under the influence. First, her cheeks were blushed. Shortly after, she took her singlet off, claiming it was way too warm, then she suggested that we listen to some music. I turned on my old iPod and just put a random playlist. She started moving to the music and singing along.

I finished my glass of wine and told her I wanted to have a shower. She said she was going to finish cooking. The kids walked into the kitchen, and as I made my way to the bathroom, I noticed Leanne started dancing with them.

When I came out of the shower, I could smell the food. Although I did not know what she had made, I smelled garlic and prawns.

Leanne told me someone had come by.

'Your friend came in, but she didn't want to wait.'

'Which friend?'

'Felicity.'

'Felicity?' I said in a much louder voice.

'Yes. Is she not a friend?'

'She is.'

'You seem shocked.'

'No. It's just that … I haven't heard from her in a long time.'

'Mmm. She seemed shocked too.'

'Really? How so?'

'I don't know. First, she asked me who I was. Then she looked me up and down like she thought I was a criminal or something.'

'Did she say something? Ask for something?'

'She had some bag. Said the kids had left clothes there. Then the kids saw her, and they looked happy to see her. They told her they wanted to show her your room.'

'My room?'

'Yes. The painting.'

'Oh. Did she like it?'

'I don't know. The kids told her that I had painted it. Then they told her I'm a tattoo artist, and lastly, that you got a tattoo.'

'Shit!'

'What?'

'Nothing. I just … Well, my tattoo was not meant to be so public. It's a private thing, you know?' I lied. 'Intimate. Anyway, It's not so bad. I just have been really busy, and she's been busy too, so I haven't seen her as much as usual. But we used to hang out a lot, and my kids are friends with her kids. You'll probably see her again a few times. So It's no big deal she heard about my tattoo. I wish I'd told her myself, that's all.'

'Oh. I see.'

'Anyway. How's that food going?'

'It's ready.'

'Then let's eat, shall we?'

'Yes.'

I wasn't drunk yet, but the thought that Felicity had come into my house for whatever reason, then did not have the decency to wait for me, really upset me. I also felt awkward about the tattoo thing, like she had found out about my news as if she'd read in some gossip magazine. Then It dawned on me: she'd seen Leanne wearing our special bikini top. I wonder if she assumed I'd given it to Leanne.

'Are you trying to remember something?'

'Pardon?'

'It's your eyes. I read about that. We tend to look upwards, slightly to one side, when we're trying to retrieve information from our memory.'

She was kind of right. I wasn't trying to remember something, but I was analysing the situation, trying to establish what Felicity was thinking and also why she had visited unannounced. And as I could not make up my mind about what to believe, I shrugged and filled up my glass.

We stayed up chatting for a bit after the kids went to bed. She asked me if I had a boyfriend.

'Over the last seven years, I have not been into men. I'm only interested in girls these days.'

'Really? I never had a lesbian friend. That's so cool. And d'you have a girlfriend?'

'No, not at the moment. Life's too busy. I want to keep my life simple. Uncomplicated.'

'I see.'

CHAPTER 9

GUILT, PRIDE AND FEAR

B iancha and I texted each other a few times. According to her, Felicity was convinced I was having some kind of affair with Leanne, but I was not. We did sleep together, twice, but that was after. I think we were just lonely, and it made sense to comfort one another at the time. Or maybe Felicity's suspicion gave me an idea.

The coronavirus had become widespread globally, and the Australian government closed the national borders. Leanne's plans to go to Ireland were put on hold. She also could not work, as the tattoo place was shut down indefinitely. Towards the end of April, she got a job at the main train station, sanitising the place.

I started therapy again after the second—and last—time Leanne and I had sex. That was still before Perth's lockdown. Somehow, I felt off and partly guilty about the intimacy with Leanne. My therapist asked me if I regretted it.

'I'm not sure.'

'If you could go back in time, would you avoid the situation? Or do you think you'd allow it to happen?'

'I think I'd probably avoid, or at least postpone it.'

'Right. When we regret, we wish we could change the past. Sadly, we can't. But you're in control of your present. Remember that. It's a powerful thought that we often underestimate. Don't you think?'

'Yes, but my regrets about the past. I'm living with guilt because of the past.'

'I can understand that. But here's a thought: our past is what can inform us. So we use it. we use the information from the past to our benefit, in the present.'

'I wish I could speak with Felicity.'

'And why don't you?'

'I don't want to give her the satisfaction.'

'Who do you think would be more satisfied? You or Felicity?'

'I don't know.'

'I'd like to try something with you. Imagine that I am Felicity. What would you say to me?'

'I'd like to ask her some questions, but then I'm scared of the answers.'

'I see. It must be really hard. What do you fear most?'

'That she slept with Tom. That she liked it. That she's been seeing him or might start seeing him.'

'What I think I'm hearing is that you are feeling angry, scared, and guilty. Do you think that's correct?'

'Yes, I suppose so. I feel hypocritical because I'm feeling like I hate the thought she may have slept with Tom, but I'm not even sure that happened. Meanwhile, I am fully aware I did sleep with someone.'

'Okay. I'm going to start with the guilt, if that's okay with you. Correct me if I'm wrong: you and Felicity have not been together for over six months.'

'That's correct.'

'I'd like to remind you that if she had sex with that man, on the night of her birthday celebration, you and Felicity were still together. I think I would feel betrayed in that hypothetical situation if I had been in your position. But, on the other hand, when you had sex with Leanne, you were no longer in a relationship with Felicity.'

'Yes, but I still have feelings for her. Like I feel I was disloyal.'

'But you are no longer together. You are free to go out with whoever you fancy. Could it be that you feel you've been disloyal to yourself?'

'I feel I gave to someone else what actually wasn't mine to give.'

'Whose was it?'

'Felicity's.'

'Maybe she needs to know that.'

'What do you mean?'

'I'd like to share an anecdote with you. May I?'

'Of course.'

'When I was a kid, about seven years old, I went away with my dad for the weekend. He had a new girlfriend, as my parents were divorced. Anyway, I was a very shy child. Dad picked me up in his car. I was by myself in the back seat when I noticed a stuffed toy. It was a cat, still in its box. I remember vividly: it wasn't really a box but a clear plastic cylinder. I looked at it and smiled. I opened the box and held the cat. I remember I gave it a name, "Potsy".

'We were in the car for about an hour. As we arrived, I picked up my little bag and left Potsy in the car. I remember I looked at him—I'd decided he was a boy, like me—and thought, *I wish he was mine,* but then I thought the right thing to do was to leave it there, rather than helping myself to someone else's property. I also remember thinking it belonged to Dad's girlfriend.

'We spent two nights in a chalet then headed back. Again, in the car, I played with Potsy. Then I put him back into the plastic cylinder. As Dad dropped me off at Mum's, I got out of the car and started saying goodbye to them. Then my dad noticed the cat, still on the seat. He then asked, "Aren't you going to take Potsy with you? Didn't you like him?" I remember I felt so happy but also so surprised. At no time had my dad said, "I got that for you," or anything to that effect. I said, "Oh, is it for me? I thought it was Kathy's."

'My point is, you may feel you belong, emotionally, to Felicity, but if she does not know that she cannot exercise that "ownership", even if she wants to. By the way, I'm using the words "ownership" and "belonging" to go along with your analogy, although I'm sure both of us know as people, we don't belong to anyone, as we're not property.

'Anyway, of course, it was much easier for my dad, as he knew for sure the cat was meant to be mine. He wasn't split between giving it to me or not, but he also made assumptions that I'd take it for granted the cat was mine. And maybe I would have, if I hadn't been so shy'

'She could ask me things directly rather than make assumptions.'

'You are right. She could ask you. Maybe the two of you are very similar in some areas.'

'What do you mean?'

'You know that she was alone with a man, who happened to be flirting with her, and you suspect, or fear, that she may have started seeing him. Felicity sees your housemate wearing a bikini top that used to have a special meaning for the two of you, then she assumes you are in some kind of relationship with your housemate. Then each of you go about your lives separately, each with your own fantasies.'

'Do you think she's angry?'

'She could be. But I'm more concerned with your feelings. Are YOU feeling angry?'

'I feel … lots of things.'

'Could you name one?'

'I feel extremely sad that I lost her. I feel angry that she was so thoughtless towards me and that she never apologised.'

'I think those are very valid reasons for the feelings you just mentioned.'

He paused, but I remained silent.

He went on. 'What would be different in your life right now for you not to be sad?'

'We'd be together.'

After my session, I went for a walk before going home, as I needed a bit of time to transition before I could interact with the kids. I tried to think about the important people in my life. I thought about my boys, then my dear friend, Dominique. She had been planning to visit me for my following birthday, but that needed to wait too.

By this time, Domi, the au pair, had managed to make her way to Tasmania. In Perth, we had to stay home, as part of our social distancing and isolation, for only about three months. It wasn't much compared to other places in the world, but it was a big thing for us.

Our lockdown started in April. Adam, my ex-husband, had travelled to South Africa in February to visit his family and got stuck there, also indefinitely. I was stuck home with my children and this eccentric lady I'd met only months before. We got to know one another a lot better. Most of the time, we got along, but there were moments in which I wanted to escape but had no choice.

Some time in late June, I returned to work after working from home for three months. That was bliss, although I never thought I'd say that. Just to be able to go somewhere else and be in the company of other people.

One day when I returned home, Leanne was in the living room watching TV. She told me she had watched seasons one to three of *The L Word*. Then she started acting really strange and saying random stuff like did I want to have another child, for instance. A few weeks later, I came home to find her holding a baby. It gave me the fright of my life!

She clearly had no idea of how to nurse a baby.

'Hi. This is Bruce.'

'Bruce?'

'Yes.'

'And Bruce is?'

'A baby.'

'Right. Well, that was kind of obvious … but …where does Bruce live?,And why is he here?'

'Oh, yes. Well, he lives just a few doors away. And I'm his babysitter. I hope you don't mind. His mum'll be picking him up soon. I thought it'd be a good opportunity for me to practice.'

'Practice what, exactly?'

'Looking after a young child. In case I have a baby.'

'Right. Of course,' I said, not quite sure of what to make of it all.

'So how's it going? Is he an easy baby?'

'I don't know.'

'You don't know?'

'I've never had one, so I can't compare. He's 10 months old. I've been told the mother has postnatal depression so they decided to get someone else to look after Bruce every day for two hours so she can have some time for herself.'

That bit of information changed my whole view of the whole thing. I felt judgemental. I thought about decades ago when the topic of postnatal depression was a taboo. I wondered how many mothers went through that undiagnosed, unassisted, unacknowledged. What would it be like for a mother to admit she is feeling miserable about having a baby? On top of dealing with the well-known symptoms of depression, the anxiety of fearing being judged and frowned upon must exacerbate it.

There are so many expectations around parenthood. I remember when it was time for me to go back to work. I did not feel it was safe to say I was a single parent at interviews. I tried hard to leave that bit of information undisclosed. Things are easier here in this regard than where I came from but the memory of how hard it is for mothers to be trusted by a potential employer, as a reliable employee, was still too fresh. Perhaps one reason is that unemployment there is a much bigger problem, due to overpopulation and other factors related to the economy.

At my boys' school, at times I felt awkward to admit I worked long hours. It's a posh school, ironically, considering it's a government school, but since it's a posh neighbourhood, many of the families living in the area have a very privileged lifestyle. With some exceptions, most families follow the more conventional model of one parent working, that generally being the male, if it's a straight couple. The other parent is expected to stay home and look after the family.

At job interviews I felt anxious about having two children, and not even having a partner. At the school I felt anxious about having a job that took me away from the 'family life' for so many hours per week. While most mums were engaged in fundraising activities and other school events, I had to work. I had to take time off in order to participate of school events such as excursions and carnivals. Some parents seemed understanding. Others not so much.

I looked at Leanne and felt admiration.

'I was reading him a story, but I'm not sure he was enjoying it.'

I glanced at the couch where she was seated and spotted an open book.

'I need to make a couple of phone calls, so I'll leave you to what you were doing. If you need any assistance, please ask.'

I left them in the living room and went to my own bedroom. I had 15 minutes before I had to pick the kids up from school. As I walked away from Leanne and Bruce, I heard her read to him nothing less than *Alice in Wonderland*.

She continued to help out with Bruce in weeks to come. I must admit she showed determination: I saw her reading some books on child minding and she even bought some baby dolls and asked me some questions.

Another day, I got home and she was reading one of my books on sexuality. After dinner, she asked me lots of questions. The interesting thing is that she was not embarrassed, not a single bit. She was always serious and often would laugh at things I would not.

That night she asked if I'd ever had a threesome. I said I had not, and she said she was thinking about trying.

'Don't worry, I won't try it here.'

'I don't mind if you try it here, so long as it's when neither the kids nor I am at home, and so long as you are extremely careful with what kind of person you bring here.'

'I think I'd prefer to do it elsewhere. I saw a movie in which something like that happened, and then one of them became a stalker. I don't want them to know where I live.'

My mind travelled fast to a time in which I was still married to Adam. We lived in a large house and there was a granny flat. When harmony was no longer possible between us, he started sleeping in the granny flat. I didn't think much of it but it did cross my mind that it was odd that he did not simply move to our spare room, in the main house.

Adam had a regular visitor, as it turns out. A nocturnal regular visitor. After he'd moved out but before the house was sold, I got a knock on my door one morning.

'Where is Amy?', this tall bulky man was asking repeatedly. With the same insistence as his question, I said I did not know any Amy and had no idea what he was talking about.

'The man in the granny flat. Where's he?'

'He no longer lives here. What has he got to do with this?'

'He paid for Amy most nights. I need to find her.'

I finally understood. I had a pimp at my door. An angry one.

'I'm sorry. I can't help you. I need to go back inside. I was making breakfast for my kids.'

'If you see him, you tell him we are looking for Amy.'

Back to the present, I continued the conversation with Leanne:

'That sounds wise. Why do you want to try it anyway, just out of curiosity?'

'I don't know. After I had my first drink with you, I realised how much I have never done. My parents brought me up as a Christian, and there were so many things we were never allowed. I think I want to break many of those rules and write my own rules again.'

'I like that idea very much. It sounds healthy.'

'I think I got tired of being told what I could and could not do and never being given an explanation that made sense to me. Everything was either *because God doesn't like it*, or *because God likes it.'*

'Which church did you belong to?'

'Baptist. Even the music we listened to was controlled. Apparently, rock is bad because it offends God.'

'You know, nowadays there are quite a few churches that are more open to modern music, more inclusive, generally speaking.'

Do you ever go to church?'

'Not anymore.'

'Which denomination did you belong to?'

'I was brought up as a Catholic. My whole family was.'

'I always wanted to be a Catholic when I was still in high school.'

'How come?'

'I wanted to confess. We weren't allowed to talk to our parents about our feelings and stuff like that, and I remember thinking at least the Catholic Church gave its followers that option, to be heard by a human being, then be absolved.'

'D'you still feel that need? To speak with someone?'

'Not as much. I have learnt to make connections outside my family nucleus, and I think I communicate better these days. Plus, I no longer feel guilty because I like listening to rock music, masturbating, or for having sex without being married.'

'I'm very glad to hear that. And if you ever feel like talking, like we are doing now, you can. Okay?'

'Okay. Thanks. You too.'

I said goodnight and went to tuck the kids into bed. I started to hear the soothing sound of the rain, which made the idea of going to bed very inviting. I stayed with them for a few minutes and then went to my own bed, with the intention of reading for a bit, but I couldn't concentrate.

I kept thinking about Felicity and wondering what it was like for her, growing up with a Christian family; whether they were strict; if she suffered for it, and if any part of her, any corner of her mind, believed that same-sex relationships were 'the devil's work'. Had her brother's story helped her empathise more? Or had it actually made her more guilt-prone? I closed my book and tried to sleep. Then I dreamed I ran into Felicity and somehow found out she was married to Tom. Out of the blue, I ask her, 'Why?'

'Because It's easy. Being in a straight relationship will always be much easier.'

I noticed she had a prominent belly and as I directed my gaze to that part of her body, then quickly shifted it to her eyes, inquisitively, she explained, 'Yes, I'm expecting. I actually think it could be yours. But I haven't told him that.'

CHAPTER 10

MEET THE PARENTS, MEET THE MISS

One morning, a few months later, I was going back home from my run when I bumped into Felicity's parents, who were leaving our local deli. They seemed happy to see me.

'Hey, long time, no see!'

'Hi Mark, hi Ophelia. How are you?'

'Yes, good. Are you busy? We'd love to have a cup of tea with you. Come over.'

'I have to prepare lunch, but I have time for a cuppa.'

'Excellent.'

We walked together to their house, and they led me inside. I'd been to their house before a few times, but never without Fli. I must admit I was slightly apprehensive.

As we walked across the living room, I saw a photo of Felicity with her children. It looked like a recent photo because the kids looked taller than I remembered. Felicity looked the same but wearing some clothes that weren't really her style. I strayed from the direction we were going and stopped to look at the photograph.

'What a lovely picture.'

'Thanks. Yes, we don't really like digital photos much. Every now and then Felicity prints some for us. The kids brought this one last time they visited'.

'I see. Well, it's lovely.'

Ophelia put the kettle on, and Mark got some cups on the table. Ophelia brought a large teapot and let it sit so the tea could brew. The three of us sat at the table and engaged in small talk for a few minutes. After all of us had our cups filled with tea, Mark managed to shift the conversation.

'Have you seen much of Felicity lately?'

'As a matter of fact, I haven't. We have been a bit busy with different things and ended up a little bit distanced.'

'We are very worried about her.'

'You are?'

'Yes.'

Ophelia, who was sitting opposite me, stretched her arms towards me, looked me in the eye and finally spoke. 'She was so much better when she was hanging out with you. You were a good influence.'

'I agree,' said Mark.

I remained silent. Mark went on. 'Clarissa, we know.'

'Pardon?'

'You don't need to hide it from us. Felicity already told us.'

'She did?'

'Yes. It's been very hard for us. But … it's the situation.'

Ophelia simply nodded, with her eyes wide open. Mark shook his head, wiped his forehead with the palm of his hand, and kept speaking. 'I think she's lost the plot.'

'Me too. I've been praying so much for her!' agreed Ophelia, at which point I was back to being totally confused.

'Have you met her, Clarissa?'

My blank face probably led them to believe I had not, but I actually did not know who they were talking about.

'Well, at least you won't be surprised like we were. Be prepared. She's awfully unpleasant. The woman looks like a bloke. Rough as guts.'

'She has no table manners,' added Ophelia. 'She burps at the table every five minutes. And that's really not the whole picture.'

'Not at all,' agreed Mark. 'Most ghastly, the whole thing. Ghastly. That she would choose someone like that for a partner, now that's a terrible thought. So we thought maybe you could help her. Get some sense back into her.'

That's how I found out Felicity had been going out with another woman AND had told her parents. This seemingly 'ghastly woman' got more than I ever did. *At least now I know she isn't with Tom*, I thought.

'You know, I feel so honoured that you trust me this much and think so highly of me, but I am not sure I can help you much. I can't change Felicity's heart.'

'And with all due respect, I want her to be happy, and if this woman brings her happiness, then she should stay with her. I'm sorry, but I need to be honest with you.'

'But she's lost her mind. She must have! This is not normal behaviour. She's drinking like a fish, and now she's smoking pot again.'

Ophelia spoke next. 'This girlfriend of hers, she has a mohawk, and her whole arm's covered in tattoos.'

'Well, some tattoos can be nice. I have one.'

'Do you? Where?'

'Mark!' Ophelia said in a reproachful tone. 'You can't ask this type of question!'

'It's okay, really. I have one tattoo, and It's on my back. It's actually relatively new.'

'Well, I bet yours is nice. Hers is like someone with a blindfold on just got a marker and scribbled all over her arm. Worse than a pirate's.'

I wanted to laugh but didn't.

'Look, try to look beyond her appearance, hard as it may be. You may find that she's nice if you give her a chance. The tattoos are really not important, nor the hairstyle.'

I was trying to reason with them, but if I'm to be honest, I was saying those words for my benefit too, as deep inside, I was surprised at the description they gave of this woman. My reaction caused me to feel shallow and judgemental, then I told myself to refocus and reminded myself that this was not about me.

Mark continued. 'But what's really worrying me is that she's going out a lot, at night, and the substance abuse, you know?

'I hope she hasn't been driving under the influence. She could even lose the custody of her children.'

At that point, I started to worry. Not only because of the kids. I worried for Felicity's wellbeing too.

'This woman is nothing but trouble. And I think Felicity is just doing this to hurt us.'

'No, Mark. She wouldn't do that.'

'You don't know that. I think she is. I think this is about her brother!'

CHAPTER 11

GINGER-BREAD HOUSE COMP

I don't think they were aware that I knew the details about Felix, only that he had passed at a very young age. Back in 2018, they had invited me for a Christmas celebration once and we decided to have a gingerbread house competition, but Felicity didn't want to be part of it. Her dad tried to persuade her, and she raised her voice and said, 'Dad, I can't. It reminds me too much of Felix,' at which point Ophelia started to cry. Felicity rose to her feet and announced, 'I need some alone time, so I'm going to his room for 10 minutes. I'll come back soon.'

I wanted to offer to go with her, but she'd said, 'alone time', so I respected that.

Mark was the first to speak. 'I'm sorry about that, Clarissa. You shouldn't have witnessed this.'

'Don't worry. It's all good. All families have these moments.'

'You are very kind,' he said as he walked towards his wife, sitting down with her and trying to offer some comfort.

Biancha was the next to speak. 'Dad, why don't you help the kids with their gingerbread house?'

As Mark got up and went away with the children, Biancha sat between her mother and me. She hugged her mum for a moment, then looked at me and explained, 'Felicity and I used to have a brother. She and him were particularly close. He passed away when she was 13. It was around Christmas time too.'

'I am really sorry to hear that. Look, if you guys want some space, I understand. I can go home.'

'Don't be silly. We've got lots of food to eat,' she said and smiled. 'And lots of drinks too.'

After the gathering at Felicity's parents', we went back to her house and stayed for the night. Once the kids were in bed, she invited me to go to the attic with her. We were halfway through the spiral staircase when she turned around and held my hands, then spoke, 'I wanna share something with you.'

'Okay!'

As we reached the top floor, she asked me to sit on the couch, and I obeyed. She walked towards the other end of the room, and I saw her open a cupboard I did not know existed. Then she pulled out a chest that was on wheels, brought it closer to where I was sitting, and she also sat down. I was curious but said nothing and waited patiently. Felicity opened the chest and removed a large box from inside. She then started to place each piece that was in the box onto the coffee table in front of us. They were miniature pieces, mostly furniture, like for a doll's house.

'Felix taught me to appreciate these things. When he was away, before his last visit, we exchanged a few letters. We had agreed to be in the same team for the gingerbread house competition that we were meant to take part in for our family's Christmas dinner. In contrast to all previous years, each team would be expected to work on their gingerbread house prior to the party, and then we'd just decide on the winner.

'So Mum and Dad were a team, Biancha was paired with her boyfriend, and I was with Felix. In one of his letters he asked me if I had any thoughts about the inside of our house, that he believed we should work on its internal aspect. At first, I laughed. I didn't see it as possible and thought he was joking. He asked if I could make some drawings of furniture, provided they were simple enough. Once we even talked about some details for the legs of our table, and I came up with the idea of a round bed.

'He told me he loved it because you could spin around at night like the hands of a clock, and no matter where you were, you wouldn't be out of place. No headboard, no foot, nothing. He said, "Brilliant! In fact, I think we should patent it.", I remember him saying.'

'Then the day he arrived in Perth, he invited me to his room and started to unpack. He removed a small box from inside his suitcase and placed it on top of his pillow. He went on unpacking, removing item by item, making sure everything was properly folded, and putting each piece in his wardrobe, but we kept talking as he tried to convince me to focus on the inside of the gingerbread house. "So, are you going to help me with the decor?" I remember I said something like, "D'you really think it'll make a difference? no one'll see this, Felix."

'He told me people wouldn't see it if it wasn't there, but that they would if it existed. I also remember he said that everything that's empty isn't even half as interesting. According to him, as soon as someone realised something was empty, they'd probably lose interest, unless they could fill it themselves.

'At first, I didn't really get what he meant. He gave me some examples. "Think of glass. Or a bottle. Either one's useless unless you have something to fill it with. The same goes for a hat. This one, for example," and he gave me a cap he'd bought for me. "It needs a head! Put it on."

'I laughed, thanked him and put the hat on. He continued, "Would you rather have an empty plate, or one filled with Mum's baked sausages? And what would be the purpose of having an empty bag unless you had something to put in it?"

'I laughed again. Then he gave me some pieces he'd been working on for our gingerbread house and boasted, "We're SO going to win this competition!"'

Felicity pointed to the items she'd displayed on the coffee table. There was a couch, a cat, a stove, a couple of pots, a few cups, a table with chairs, a rug, a lamp, and a round bed with pillows, which is how you could tell it was indeed a bed and not a table. I gently touched them, one by one, and noticed they were made of clay, except for the rug.

'They're really, really cute, Fli.'

'Felix asked me to colour them. He said he trusted my taste for colours better. But before I could paint them, he was gone.'

'The cat's painted.'

'Yes, that one was easy. Felix had a cat. Snowpaws. In fact, Felix asked me to look after it when he left Perth to the boarding school.'

The miniature cat was painted black with white paws. Its tail was up.

We remained silent for a brief moment, and she continued, 'So in the end, I kept the rest of them as he gave them to me. This way I can look at them and imagine. Different possibilities.'

'Is that where you take your inspiration for your work?'

'Maybe. I don't know. I do know I had him in mind when I designed this house. I couldn't design our gingerbread house, so I designed this one instead. I wanted him to be proud. This attic, for instance. It's very much based on what we discussed for the gingerbread house: sloped walls, clear front so the furniture could be seen … Nowadays I always ask him for help when I have a project. He never lets me down.'

She picked up the miniature cat between her thumb and her finger index: 'Meet feline Felix Snowpaws.'

'Hi, Felix!'

Felicity smiled, then looked me in the eye, as if she wanted to say something.

'What are you thinking about, Fli?'

'Nothing much.'

'Please share.'

'I was just thinking that … I never showed this to anyone else. I think apart from Felix, you're the only one who gets me.'

I hugged her, and after a brief moment, I suggested we go to bed.

We had already got changed and were in bed. I was about to fall asleep when she whispered, 'Clar?'

I took longer than usual to reply because she'd had never called me by that name before.

'Yes?'

'If we ever live together, would you mind …?'

'What? Living together? Of course not!'

'No. I meant something else. But It's good you wouldn't mind living together.'

'Is it now?' I said, half-joking.

'Yes.'

'So what did you mean then? Would I mind what?'

'If we had a cat.'

First, I chuckled. Then I held her closer to me and kissed her gently. Even though it was dark, I could see her silhouette. Finally, I replied, 'Of course not. There'll be a Felix in the family again. Not sure about the white paws, though. Might be a tad hard to find.'

Chapter 12

Who's in Danger?

That was one and a half years before. Now I was having tea with her parents and discussing her relationship with a woman.

'Look, I don't think you should take it personally. Felicity is probably just following her heart.'

'No, she's not. Unless her heart is filled with revenge. She's trying to avenge her brother.'

Ophelia butted in at the words 'her brother'. 'It's like she wants to be Felix.'

'That sounds very Shakespearean,' I said.

Their blank faces informed me that they totally missed my attempt at a joke, but even that was better than the path the conversation was taking.

'Look, I can understand you are worried but just give her some space.'

'She's self-destructive right now.'

'She ... has a good head on her shoulders,' I assured them.

'Yes, she used to. But I think this woman has taken that away from her. She's a terrible, terrible influence. Please have a word with her. Maybe invite her to go somewhere nice, introduce her to some of your friends. Anyone would be better than this troll.'

By that time, I had formed a horrible idea about this woman and wished I never crossed paths with her.

I went home in no mood to cook dinner. I had a hot shower, got changed and decided to get fish and chips. The boys were super happy. I opened a bottle of wine and had a couple of drinks with Leanne. She talked to me about religion and philosophy, and then we ended up talking about friendship.

I wanted to have someone's opinion. 'Would you try to interfere in a very close friend's life if you thought they were in danger?'

'Only if I was sure they were indeed in danger.'

'How do you mean?'

'Well, define "danger".'

'Something that puts your wellbeing at risk.'

'Okay, then yes. But only if I knew it was not just gossip. So, say I heard a rumour. Then I'd ask my friend. If we were friends, then I would feel comfortable enough to ask. Just be upfront. Like with you, for instance. Sometimes I want to say things to you, but then I think It's none of my business, and I don't feel you are in danger, so I say nothing.'

'What d'you mean? What do you want to say to me?'

'Well, I thought about saying that you should let go of your past. Whoever hurt you can no longer hurt you. I thought of saying that you should try to move on. But then I thought that this is easily said. I myself can't let go of the past, well, part of it. So I suppose we all have our time and deal with things at our own pace. So maybe your friend needs to have their arse kicked, or maybe they just need some time to figure things out.'

CHAPTER 13

A KISS

Another Christmas went by, and it still felt rather different not to spend it with Felicity. The year before, nearly six months after her birthday party, she'd travelled with the children. In a way, that made it much easier for me to explain to my twins why we were not all celebrating together. When they asked the following Christmas, I pretended it was because of Covid-19. They didn't seem convinced but accepted it. Then the year ended. Eventually, Felicity and I started socialising more often again, but obviously not as frequently as before, and only with things to do with the children. Whether it was fate or a deliberate choice from either of us, we never had the opportunity to be together alone. I think I liked it that way. It was important to me to keep my distance and protect myself. I particularly feared meeting her girlfriend. In fact, I dreaded the idea of being introduced to her and could not think of a more humiliating situation for me. Luckily, it never happened.

The twins and I were invited to Lola's birthday party a few months ago. Felicity's girlfriend was not there, so I assumed it was probably not her kind of fun.

Biancha and I had a coffee together at the birthday party, away from the other guests, who were mostly children, but there were a few parents, because Felicity being Felicity, she extended the invitation to three of Charlie's friends, so he'd have some company of a similar age to his. As we talked, Biancha insinuated I should try to get back together with Fli.

'Your sister is in a relationship already, and she isn't interested in me.'

'I think you're wrong.'

'About which part?'

'About her feelings for you.'

'Well, she just let me go very easily and never looked back.'

'She was ashamed.'

'So was I.'

'She actually thinks you and Leanne are happy, and she feels she would be destroying something good. I reckon she's only been dating this woman because that was how she found the courage to tell Mum and Dad.'

I felt my blood boil and had to exercise a lot of self-control in order not to yell.

'Wow! What a compliment. She finally finds the strength with someone who apparently doesn't mean much to her … Is this supposed to make me feel good? Anyway, I don't even know why I'm talking about this. And her concern about destroying something good? Well, in case she hasn't realised, she's already destroyed something good: she destroyed us. What a load of rubbish! What does she know about Leanne? She probably saw her once, then made lots of assumptions. Why did she not even ask me? Okay, maybe she saw her a few times from a distance … Maybe she said hello a couple of times when she came to pick Lola up at our place, but to say we are together, really!'

Biancha was able to keep calm. She listened to my every word patiently and when I'd finished, she rested her right hand on my left shoulder and looked into my eyes. As she spoke, her voice sprayed compassion.

'She met up with Leanne very recently, actually. She rang her because Leanne left a message on her phone. Leanne wanted Fli to help her organise a surprise birthday party for you. Fli told her that you did not like birthday parties, and Leanne gave up on the idea. But they met for a coffee, and Leanne spoke about you all the time, and how her life had changed, how she'd learned to drink, how she for the first time thought being a mother wasn't totally out of her capability … and how it felt like a family, blah-blah-blah. And she asked Fli to help her choose a present for you.'

I was speechless.

Biancha continued. 'And she said to Fli that she was certain that someone had broken your heart, but that you never spoke about it, and that she thought it must have been your ex-husband, and that she thought that was why you turned to women. She kind of asked Fli if she knew anything she could share. Fli said she wasn't comfortable discussing that with her, and then Leanne apologised and changed the topic.'

At that moment, Fli came over and asked if she could sit with us. She looked as dazzling as always. She stood still in front of me, one hand inside the back pocket of her olive green cargo pants, something I'd noticed her do many times and generally associated with her being uncertain about something, or a tad nervous before saying something. Her other hand was holding a handbag. She smiled at me, and I melted, feeling almost like I was being kissed.

'It's very nice to have you here.'

'Thank you.'

'I have an extra lolly bag for you. Here, you can have yours earlier.' She took a fabric bag from inside her handbag and gave it to me. Inside there was a mask—the party was all themed around Coronavirus—some lollies in the shape of the virus, a mini bottle of alcohol gel, and a bar of soap. I laughed, then I noticed she was observing my reaction.

'Thank you.'

'You're welcome. I can't believe It's been almost two years.'

'Me neither.'

'I don't even remember much about last year, but I wanted to say that … if I did not invite you to celebrate with us or if I did not show up much, it was because … I was probably not very sociable at the time.'

'Nobody was. We had a lockdown, remember?'

'Oh yes! That's making more sense now … among other … things …and reasons.'

'Such as?'

'Such as me never receiving a thank you or just an acknowledgement of the flowers I sent you two years ago … Or my singing telegram.'

My blood started boiling again.

'Oh that? Yes, thank you. Thank you so much for sending some barefoot vagabond to tell me that all you wanted, no, listen to this, ALL you wanted was some romance.'

I turned my head to face Biancha, who in turn, looked down. Felicity continued.

'Oh come on! You are being petty. That is not what I meant.'

'Wasn't it? Because that's what your hippy friend sang. And you know what? Maybe when you have something to tell me, you should say it yourself, to my face. But when you choose not to, don't blame your messenger. Was it you who wrote all the lyrics to your masterpiece poetry?'

'I did. In the attic. As stated,'

Biancha interrupted. 'Hummm.' She cleared her throat and continued, 'Is it time for the cake? Let's sing happy birthday and have some cake.'

With her eyes still locked into mine, she replied:

'I'm going to have a cigarette first. Then, when I come back, we can cut the cake.'

I was surprised because she'd stopped smoking two months before her big birthday party, two years before.

'I thought you had quit.'

'I had. I just started again a while ago. Actually, it was the day I went to your house and found out your new lover had tattooed your back.'

I didn't have the stamina to prolong the conversation. I didn't manage to set things straight and tell her it had not been Leanne who'd tattooed me, nor to say that Leanne and I were not lovers.

I didn't have any cake but was given some to take home. Felicity walked with me and the kids to my car and waited for us to get in. Lola and my twins were whispering, then my boys started to ask if they could have a sleepover at Felicity's, and although I wasn't really warming up to the idea, she assured me it was okay by her. I argued that we had not packed toothbrushes nor pyjamas, nor anything.

'I still have their stuff. We have toothbrushes for them at home permanently. And pyjamas too.'

I felt disconcerted, as I did not have the same for her children. I had spare toothbrushes, but not some toothbrushes set aside specifically for them.

I looked down, then I looked up at her. 'Thanks. I'll pick them up in the morning if you let me know when they're up.'

She just nodded and smiled. I got out of the car with the kids, then hugged them, said bye, told them I loved them and asked them to behave. They ran away back to the party with Lola and I got into the car again. I had my window down, and as I was about to turn the ignition on, Felicity lowered her head, getting it level with mine and spoke. 'I'm sorry.'

'For what?'

'That I didn't live up to your expectations. Looking back, I realise the bar was … too high for me.'

Without any warning, she kissed me, and I offered no resistance. She pulled away gently, said goodbye and walked away.

CHAPTER 14

LET'S TALK

I f I thought that the events of Lola's party were surprising and had impacted me, I had no idea what was about to come. A few weeks later, I received a phone call from Biancha. She said she was outside my place, in her car, and asked whether I was home, and would I come outside.

'Would you like to come in for a cuppa?'

'Thanks, but I'm in a bit of a rush.'

So I got into her car, as it was raining.

'Sorry to come unannounced.'

'Don't worry about that. What's up?'

'D'you still have Felicity's spare keys?'

'As a matter of fact, I do. Does she want them back?'

'No. Well, I don't know. Could you go there and check on her? I'm worried.'

'Sure. But what's happened?'

'Please grab the keys. I'll tell you on the way.'

I ducked inside and was back in no time.

Biancha started to explain. 'She rang me randomly and asked if she could leave the kids with me for the day, as "something had come up" and she needed to go somewhere for a good few hours. I said yes and she dropped them off. I told her they could stay for the night and that we might watch a movie together. That was about 10 am. I took the kids to the museum then we had lunch, went to the park and came back home because the rain started. They wanted to play Monopoly, but I don't own a set. So I said I could check if Felicity was home, and if she was, I could get their Monopoly. Lola said, "You can still get it if Mum's not there. It's in the shed."

I remember their shed. Felicity turned it into a playroom.

'I did not want the kids to come with me, in case Felicity was ... entertaining, you know?'

I nodded.

'So I made up an excuse and dropped them at Mum and Dad's for a while and went to Fli's.'

As we arrived at Felicity's, and Biancha turned the ignition off, I could hear some music coming from the house.

'Sounds like she's home.'

'Well, that's the problem. When I came 20 minutes ago, I could hear the same song. Then I assumed she was home, and thought she was with someone, so I walked to the back, went into the shed and picked a few games. Then I noticed the same song started, which I found odd, so I went to my car and put the games in the boot and waited for the song to end. When it did, it started again. So I went to the front door and knocked, then banged. I rang her, but her phone's turned off. Mum and Dad also have a spare set of keys but I didn't want to involve them at this stage.'

'Okay. So what's the plan?'

'One of us goes in, the other stays in the car. I think you should go in because the keys are yours.'

'What if she's with her girlfriend?'

'She's not with Fay.'

'How d'you know that?'

'Because I rang her.'

'Okay. I'll go in. Wait for my call or text.'

The same song, which by the way was *Careless Whispers* by George Michael, was still playing, very loud. I unlocked the front door and walked in. As I reached the living room, I announced myself with a "hello", but got no answer. I decided to walk towards the source of the sound, which seemed to be the theatre room. As I got there, I saw Felicity sitting in front of the screen, which was connected to her laptop and was displaying a slide show of photos. Some of them were of us, some of her kids, some of her kids and mine, and some of her folks. There were some really old ones, and for the first time I saw Felix, or at least I assumed it was him.

I texted Biancha and said Felicity was safe, then I said I'd ring her later and that I'd walk home. I remained looking at Felicity. I noticed a pipe on the coffee table, and two bottles of wine, one empty and one full. There was only one wine glass in sight, which was in her hand. I waited for the song to end again, then before it could restart, I spoke. 'Hi.'

She moved with a startle and asked what I was doing there. She turned the music down with the remote and I explained. 'I'm sorry. I didn't mean to frighten you. Your sister asked me to check on you. She was worried.'

'Why?'

'Your music could be heard from outside. Clearly. And It's on repeat. She wanted to grab the Monopoly game for the kids and well, she thought the whole music thing was odd.'

We both remained silent for a brief moment until I stretched my arm towards her and walked in her direction. 'I never returned your keys. Here they are.' I knelt down and offered the keys with my hand open. She placed her right hand under mine then gently rested her wine glass on the floor. With her free hand, she wrapped my own hand around the keys.

'I would like you to keep them. Would you like yours back?'

I shook my head and we remained staring at one another. I put the keys back into my handbag.

'Would you like a drink?'

I thought that was rather tempting but decided I wanted and needed to be sober, so I declined. She rose to her feet and invited me to do the same, still holding my hand. She started dancing to the music, and I danced with her. After that song ended, I asked if we could pick a different playlist. She laughed and put a random playlist on.

'Would you like to watch the sunset with me from the attic?'

'Sure. But I need to ring home and make sure the kids are okay.'

'You do that. I'll wait for you upstairs.'

I rang Biancha and said Felicity had clearly had a bit too much to drink, and I did not want to leave her on her own until I was sure she was okay. She got my hint straight away and suggested my boys join Charlie and Lola for the night. I said that would be extremely helpful. I rang Leanne and told her I would not be home for dinner and asked if I could speak with the boys.

'Hi guys. I'm with Fli. She's not feeling very well so I'm looking after her and I'm going to be a while. Her sister asked me to invite you boys to her place for a sleepover as she has Charlie and Lola with her.'

They were thrilled, so I organised all the logistics with them over the phone.

After I finished making the necessary arrangements, I joined Felicity in the attic. *Piano Man* was playing. She had brought two glasses and a bottle of my favourite wine,

Rutini, a Malbec. In front of us was a wide glass pane facing west. The sky was changing, as if there was an invisible hand spray-painting it in slow motion, with a few hues of pink and orange, despite the prominent presence of grey.

Felicity started to uncork the wine.

'Fli, how much have you had to drink today?'

She shrugged then replied in a casual tone, 'Probably too much but still not enough.'

'Are you sure you want to have another glass?'

'I'd like to have another bottle, please.'

'Be serious!'

'I haven't had a drink with you in two years, just about.'

'Okay, I'll have one drink with you. But then that's it.'

We drank a glass and I convinced her to eat something. We ordered food and kept chatting. I wanted to make sure she was okay, so I asked why she was home alone drinking.

'But I'm not. I'm with you!' she joked. 'All right. I just wanted some time for myself. Haven't had that for a while. I felt I didn't have the energy to be a mum tonight. I wanted to be by my lonesome for a bit.'

'Well, I'm glad for you then. Would you like me to leave?'

'Absolutely not!'

'You can be left by your lonesome again later. I'd like to be convinced you are okay first.'

After a while, I told her I should go home. She put George Michael on again, same song, and asked me to dance again. As we danced, she burst into tears.

'I don't want you to go.'

'Felicity, is something wrong?'

'Please don't go.'

'Okay, I won't go yet. Talk to me.'

When she was no longer crying, I ventured another question. 'I'm sorry to ask this but where's your girlfriend?'

'I no longer have one.'

'Is this what all this is about? Are you asking me to stay here because you are feeling lonely after your breakup?'

She chuckled, then she started laughing and shaking her head.

'No, this is definitely not what all this is about.'

She started laughing again and then she looked me in the eye. 'I thought you knew me better than that.'

'Better than what?'

'You really think I'd use you to comfort me, so I'd feel better about having broken up with someone else?'

'Well, I also thought I knew you better, until you stood me up at your party and decided to stay with some ex-boyfriend of yours rather than come home with me, as we'd planned.'

'That was such a long time ago. I can't believe we're still talking about this.'

I raised my voice. 'We never have! After nearly two years we've never talked about this. So don't give me this shit now. With all due respect, it sounds a bit like your parents.'

'You're right. Okay, let's do this.' She paused for a moment, pressed the tip of the fingers of each hand together, took a deep breath and exhaled through her mouth then went on. 'So that night, what I did … it was a big mistake.'

'Did you sleep with him?'

'What? No! Did you really think that?'

'Well from my perspective you left me to stay partying with a guy.'

'Clarissa, no. No. I did not sleep with Tom. Neither that night nor after.'

'Did you want to?'

'For fuck's sake. No. Okay? No! En-Oh-No!'

She took a sip of wine, then as if having an afterthought, she took another one, emptying her glass. 'How can you think that?' She shook her head while looking at me.

'Don't try and turn the table, all right?' I saw how he grabbed your hand as I left. I turned back to look at you one more time, hoping you'd change your mind and come with me. You weren't even looking my way. You were looking at him, and smiling, and he grabbed your hand, and you let him.'

'Holding someone's hand is not really a big deal, Clarissa.'

'Really? It always was for you when you were with me.'

'I was drunk that night.'

'Funny how you were never drunk enough to hold MY hand in public. Anyway, sorry if I offended you. So you were saying you didn't fancy him.'

'That's right. I did not fancy Tom.'

'Then why?' I had been trying to control my emotions with all my strength but I felt tears rolling down my cheeks, which I quickly wiped away. I waited for her to reply.

'I realise that was wrong.'

'D'you have any idea what it was like for me? How I felt? What I thought?'

'I think I do have an idea, but perhaps you can tell me, so I know for sure.'

'I felt like rubbish, ditched. Like I was a commodity you decided to upgrade to the next model. I felt lost, useless, abandoned, lonely, unloved and unlovable. As time went by, I felt broken. For the first time in my life, as a mother, I doubted my capacity to be a good mum. Luckily, I had Domi to give me a hand. Only God and I know the effort I made to just keep going to work and live my life as if everything was okay. I ended up being diagnosed with PTSD and still have the odd panic attack. Occasionally, I also have nightmares about you and me and Tom.'

We were both silent for a bit. She looked down and remained pensive. I rose to my feet.

'Please don't go. I haven't finished. I still want to answer your question.'

'I'm not going. I just think I could do with another drink.'

'Make that two, will you?' she said as she handed me her empty glass.

I returned with the bottle and our two glasses.

'Listen, I want to continue this conversation, but I'm aware it's getting late, and I've had quite a bit to drink, and I'm still drinking, so I may not make it home. Is it okay if I crash on your couch?'

She smiled.

'You don't need to ask me that. Of course it's okay. You can sleep in the spare room. Or anywhere you like.'

'Thanks. I just don't want to take it for granted.'

'Okay. So, going back to our conversation. Firstly, thank you for sharing about how it was for you. I think it was good for me to hear that. Hard, but good. It hurts me to know you suffered so much. It also hurts me to know I caused it. I'm so sorry. And by that, I don't mean I'm asking for your forgiveness. All I want is for you to know that I am truly sorry.'

I nodded and she sighed.

'You asked me why I didn't go home with you on the night of my party.'

'Yes. Please enlighten me. If you didn't want to sleep with him, why the fuck did you stay?'

'It wasn't because I wanted to be with him. I stayed because I couldn't bear …' she took another deep breath and exhaled slowly… 'because it was very hard to look at you. I'd realised that I was not as strong as I'd hoped. I had planned to tell my parents and friends I was in a same-sex relationship, with you, and when the time came, I just couldn't do it. I knew I was letting you down. I knew how much the whole coming-out thing meant to you and you'd been waiting for so long, Clarissa. But I couldn't do it then, and at the time, I felt I'd never be able to come out of the closet. I didn't think you'd understand. Or accept. I thought you'd leave me. Probably because I'd have left myself. So I was also too embarrassed of myself. Ashamed. It was easier to get drunk and stay with Tom. I used him. He was just a tool. And I felt unworthy of you.'

She topped up her glass again and offered to fill up my glass. I accepted. She lifted her glass and said, 'Cheers!'

'To what?'

'To the truth.'

'To the truth.' We each took a sip, and I continued. 'Which reminds me, you know you'll be hungover in the morning, right?'

'Like that matters.'

'What d'you mean?'

'Never mind. I'm quitting anyway.'

'Drinking?'

'And smoking.'

'How come?'

'Mmm ... that's another story. Let's finish the one we started first. Is there anything else you'd like to ask? Or add?'

'Yes. Did you deliberately decide to end things between you and me?'

She brushed her hair with her hand from her forehead towards the back and looked upwards as if she was casting her memory back.

'Not at the beginning. I was confused. Part of me hoped you'd try to contact me. When you didn't, I started telling myself that you would probably be better off with someone else. Then when I found out about Leanne, I was devastated. I was angry at myself, then at my parents, so I wanted to hurt them. I met Fay, who seemed to embody just about everything my parents disliked: she was very ... unconventional.'

'So I heard.'

'Which brings me to my next point: I broke up with Fay only a few days ago, simply because I realised she was just a distraction. I don't want to be distracted anymore.'

'Well, I don't know what to say. I hope you can focus on whatever it is you'd like to.'

'Thanks.'

'No thank you, for sharing all that.'

'That's okay. Anyway, how's everything going with Leanne?'

'Fine. She's a good housemate.'

'Com'on. You know that's not what I mean.'

'Felicity, Leanne and I are not romantically involved. She really is just my housemate.'

'Yeah, right. And she was wearing the bikini we bought together because you are just housemates. And then she decorated your love nest with cupids, and to finish off, tattooed your back. But sure, I believe you're not fucking each other. I don't know why you're trying to deny it. You don't owe me anything.'

'It's just a coincidence that she's a tattoo artist. She didn't do my tat.'

'She didn't?'

'No. And the bikini … that was an accident. She didn't own bathers, so I threw all mine on the bed and told her to pick one, to borrow. She picked ours, and I felt embarrassed to say she couldn't choose that one. The painting on my wall, well, It's not a painting about cupids. Cupid's there because he's a character from ancient mythology.'

She started crying again. For a while, I just watched and waited a bit before speaking.

'Why are you crying?'

'Time,' she said as she wiped off her tears.

'What about time?'

'We waste so much time with unimportant things. Time that we don't have.'

She stood up and asked me to join her outside, as she wanted to smoke. The rain had stopped, but the seats were still wet, so we stood by the edge of the porch, leaning against the handrail. She smoked two cigarettes and we were almost silent the whole time. A flock of birds flew together right in front of us. It was one of those very unique, unforgettable moments. She was the first to speak. 'So the reason I asked you to stay with me tonight is the same reason I'm going on the wagon. By the way, this was my last cigarette. Remind me, in case I forget. I mean tomorrow.'

'Okay. So what's this reason?'

And that's when she told me she'd been diagnosed with lung cancer. I asked a few questions and she replied to all of them. I excused myself and said I needed to go to the toilet. I walked into the bathroom and after I closed the door behind me, I leaned against the door and started crying. I allowed myself to get it out of my system, then washed my face and headed towards the back porch, where we were before. She'd come inside.

'Look, if you'd rather go home, I understand.'

I shook my head held her hands then kissed them.

'I'm so sorry, Felicity.'

'For what?'

'For your sad news.'

'Well, it is what it is.'

'Who else knows?'

'Apart from my doctor? No one.'

I didn't stay on the couch or the guest room. We went to bed together and she fell asleep in no time, unlike me.

Early in the morning I messaged Biancha to check if she was up. I told her I'd pick the kids up about nine o'clock and asked if she wanted to have a coffee with us somewhere. She texted back straight away saying that was a great idea.

I walked to the bathroom and had a shower. When I returned to the bedroom, Felicity was awake. She greeted me. 'Good morning.'

I sat next to her, still wrapped in a towel, hugged her tight and whispered good morning back.

'How's your head?'

'Aching.'

'Thought so. I'll bring you some water. Let me put some clothes on first.'

'I still have some of your clothes here. Check the top drawer on the left. In case you want to wear something fresh.'

I smiled and thanked her. As I opened the drawer, I saw it was filled with my own clothes. They were all very nicely folded and piled by type. There was also a round soap in a fabric bag, which left a very pleasant scent.

After I got dressed, I went to the kitchen and got a glass of water and a Berocca® tablet. I gave it to Felicity and invited her to have a coffee with the kids, Biancha and me. At first, she said she would probably stay, but I insisted, and told her I did not want her to be on her own.

'But I have a headache.'

'Stay in bed for bit more. I'll check on you in an hour.'

'Where are you going?'

'I feel like making myself a cup of tea if that's okay with you.'

'Knock yourself out.'

I left her on her own and went into the kitchen to make a tea, then I sat by the breakfast bar, just trying to anchor myself to the present and not be anxious. Felicity walked in about an hour after. She had also showered and was wearing very nice overalls, which were dark denim with roses embroidered. She'd platted her hair. I wasn't expecting her to come so soon, so I was a bit startled, both because of the unexpected arrival and because of how gorgeous she looked.

'Sorry. Did I give you a fright?'

'No, It's okay. You just look stunning and last time I looked at you, you were looking wasted.'

We laughed. She said she was feeling much better, so she had decided to come with me to meet the others.

I helped her tidy up her living room and kitchen, took the rubbish out, and we left in her car.

When we arrived I had nodded off and she woke me. 'Hey, we're here. Did you sleep at all? Last night?'

'I did, but probably not enough.'

'I'm sorry. Did I snore?'

I laughed and shook my head.

'Have you given any thought about when you're going to tell your family?'

'Some time soon.'

The two of us got inside then shortly after we all walked to a cafe a couple of blocks away. The coffee was splendid and helped me stay awake. When it was time to go, Felicity made a suggestion. 'Clarissa, I'm thinking I could drive you home, and the kids could stay with Biancha until I get back. Then I'll take Reuben and Rupert home with us Merzs. I can return them to you later in the afternoon. This way you sleep a bit. What d'you say?'

'Yes, sure. If the boys want to stay, that could work. But isn't Biancha tired too?'

'I'm fine,' said Biancha.

'Okay, that's settled. I'll drive you then. I just need to use the toilet first when we get to B's.' We walked back to Biancha's. While the kids stayed in the garden and Felicity excused herself and walked to the bathroom, Biancha stood next to me and grilled me. 'So you had a late night, huh?'

'Yes.'

She kept staring at me as if trying to read my mind.

'Did you mmm share the same bed?'

'We did.'

'YES!'

'Both fully clothed, though.'

'What? Why?'

'Well, it wasn't really about that. Last night was about having a meaningful conversation, listening, and being present. Plus we were very tired.'

Felicity returned, we said goodbye and left. As she dropped me off, she got out of the car and gave me a hug.

'Thank you for your company, especially last night. It meant a lot to me.'

'Not at all. I enjoyed it too.'

'In the past I probably would have avoided you today, being the day after such an intense conversation.'

'That's wonderful. You've grown. Well done.'

'It's good to feel close to you again, like we can talk and we don't have to avoid one another. So I think my point is ... don't be a stranger. But I also want to say that right now, I don't have the energy for more than this. Like, I can't even think about a relationship.'

'Hey, don't stress!'

'I just don't want to disappoint you. Again.'

'Have I done or said anything that made you feel pressured? About us?'

'No. I think It's just that ... there was this two-year hiatus and then everything that was not said over months and months got said in one night.'

'That's right. And It's a lot to process. For both of us. But you need to focus on your health. And the children. I'm not interested in being in a relationship anyway.'

'You're not?'

'No,' I lied. 'I'm really enjoying being single. Simple and uncomplicated, you know?'

'Sounds good. Eventually you'll meet someone nice.'

'Who knows?! Maybe.'

'Well, I'd better go. Have some sleep. Ring me when you're up and I'll drop the boys off for you.'

'Thanks. See'ya.'

CHAPTER 15

BOUNDARIES

F elicity told Biancha about her health condition that same day. Her surgery was scheduled for the twentieth of May, which was in just over a week's time. I spoke with her often but we didn't meet for the whole week. We agreed to go for a walk on Friday after dropping the kids off, as I only had work in the afternoon.

'Are you sure you can walk?'

'Yes, I'm positive. If we walk slowly, I'll be fine.'

'Shall we walk to my place and have a cup of tea?'

'That'd be nice.'

As we got in, she removed her shoes and stood still then looked around. She inhaled slowly and deeply, looked at me and smiled.

'What are you doing?'

'Recalling some memories. I haven't been inside your place for a long time.'

'It's not very different from back then.'

Leanne was out, so Felicity and I were on our own. We sat by the kitchen table drinking tea and chatting.

'I'm surprised you're having tea so often, Clarissa. You used to be a coffee person.'

'I still am. But I figured coffee might trigger your craving for a fag. So I drink tea. It's easy.'

She remained silent, staring at me.

'What? Did I say something wrong?'

'Not at all. I was just ... surprised. You have that gift. Your thoughtfulness.'

'It's no big deal. Anyway, d'you miss it much? Smoking?'

'I haven't missed it as much as I thought, but it's only been one week. In fact, less. Today is day six. But tell me a bit about you. Are you still working for the same two places?'

'Yes, I am. I got a promotion too.'

'Well done! Tell me more.'

'Well, now I'm in charge of a team, which basically means I train some people and supervise them.'

'And d'you like it?'

'I do. It's mentally stimulating.'

'Awesome. What else? Are you still going to the gym?'

'Not really. I started running.'

'Wow. That's cool. Do you do it with a group?'

'Just me.'

'Isn't that boring?'

'No. As a matter of fact, I find it therapeutic. I do so much thinking when I'm running. If I had someone next to me, that would not be possible.'

She steered the conversation and finally managed to ask me what she really wanted to know.

'So have you met girls? Like, have you brought anyone home?'

'If what you are asking is whether I had sex with anyone, the answer is yes.'

'Good for you.'

Her facial expression was neutral so I could not tell whether she was relieved or saddened. She went on.

'So … you meet every now and then?'

'No. It was just a couple of one-night-stands. What about you? any hook-ups before Fay?'

'Nuh.'

'Plans for after?'

'I haven't been feeling much sexual desire, to be honest. Maybe It's because of my health. Not sure. But it's like I'm frigid. Probably. But you're not sick. Why don't you join a dating app?'

'You know what? I'm not sure I'm comfortable discussing this with you. I'm not ready for this. I know we said we're going to be friends but I'm not ready to talk about having sex with other people in a matter-of-fact manner when both of us are still healing from our break-up. I can handle any other topic but not this type of conversation. What's next? Are you going to tell me how much pleasure you had with your ex?'

She cleared her throat and swallowed. 'I'm sorry. I didn't mean to upset you. I just ... would like to see you happy. If I die soon, it'd be so much easier to know that you're ... settled.'

'Easier for whom? Anyway, I AM happy. Okay? You don't need to organise my life.'

'Okay.'

We finished our tea and went outside to sit in the sun for a bit. I asked her about her parents' reaction and what arrangements she had in place for her children. She told me her mum had reacted particularly badly. She also said the children would be moving in with her parents until she could return home.

CHAPTER 16

A MOTHER'S PRAYERS

F elicity went into surgery to have the pulmonary nodule removed. After the procedure, she stayed in the ICU under observation, with the idea to move into a hospital room while receiving prophylactic radio and chemotherapy. She chose to have her treatment as an in-patient to avoid the kids seeing her.

Within four to six weeks, she'd lost a quarter of her weight. She still looked like an angel to me. I visited her most days since the op. There were some complications, so she stayed in the ICU for longer than expected. While she was in the ICU, I went to the hospital every day early in the morning. A couple of times I had to wait because only one person at

123

a time was allowed in, and her family also visited when they could. We didn't always coordinate our timetable. One day, as I was told her dad was in the ICU with her, I went into the cafeteria and stayed there drinking coffee and reading for a bit. Biancha and Ophelia walked in but didn't notice me. I was sitting on a couch. They ordered their drinks and sat at a table behind my couch. I did not intend to eavesdrop but it was impossible not to overhear the conversation:

'Mum, I'm sorry but that isn't something that interests me.'

'You're being selfish. Think about your sister.'

'I am thinking about her. That's why I'm here, to support her. Look, I think It's great that you enjoy going to church. That gives you comfort and peace, and hope. But I don't believe in any of that.'

'Biancha, Felicity needs more prayer. This disease is probably a warning. A punishment from God. At least she's no longer with a woman. I hope she's asked for forgiveness. Anyway, in my Prayer Group, we have all been praying for her. I told your father. I said, "Mark, we need to have faith. Jesus will do His work." And was I right?! The doctor says the operation went well. I am so relieved she stopped seeing that woman. How could she do that to her children?'

'Mum, Felicity did not do anything to her children.'

'Come to church with me, Biancha. Come back to the faith. It's still time. God's merciful. He'll forgive Felicity. But we must pray and maybe she'll join us too. Maybe when this is all over, she can work things out with Philip and everything will be like it should.'

'For goodness' sake, Mum, will you shut the fuck up?' Biancha had raised her voice. 'I'm so sick of this rubbish! Felicity's poor health has NOTHING to do with God, nor with her sexuality. The success of the operation was not because of God's mercy nor because of your prayers. And it was not God who helped you find your glasses when you lost them last night either. If there is a God, I am sure He has much more important things to concern himself with and he wouldn't give a fuck about your glasses!'

'Watch your language.'

'No, you watch yours! Stop behaving like a delusional bitch and engage with reality.'

'I'll pray for you too. I hope you are not the next to be punished by God.'

'How dare you? I've had enough of this shit. Enjoy your coffee.'

I heard a chair moving on the floor followed by what I then confirmed were Biancha's footsteps. I thought about Felix and wondered what it would have been like growing up in that household.

CHAPTER 17

FAINTING

Once Felicity was moved into a hospital room, it was much easier to visit her, as there were fewer restrictions. Before the operation, as I was planning to be involved in her treatment, I had a conversation with Leanne and explained that Felicity was going to start a treatment and that would impact on my time. I told her that I would need to make arrangements for the kids and that the easiest solution for me would be to find a new au pair, but that I would be happy to make an arrangement with her, if she wanted to stay living with us. She was keen to stay and started taking the kids to school and picking them up when needed. I took a week off work initially, to coincide with the date of the operation, then some additional days, although not in a row. It became a routine to stop at the hospital every morning before work. If Felicity was asleep, I'd leave a note. I also tried to visit her in the evening. I particularly enjoyed bringing food for her. I'd sit on one of the two chairs that were in the room and we'd chat, mostly about the kids.

On her second week of treatment, she decided to shave her hair off. Her weight loss was also noticeable. She was cheerful and in a good mood most of the time. The only thing she ever complained about was missing the children. She video-called them regularly. I saw them at least twice a week and tried to help as much as possible.

I read a myriad of articles about cancer treatment. I was particularly worried about the effects of the chemo, which is known for being very debilitating. I expected Felicity to be very fragile by the end of the third week but to my surprise, she showed a lot of resilience.

One particular night when I arrived at the hospital, her dad was about to leave. Biancha had her back to me and was sitting on a chair by the bed, holding Felicity's hands. Since the door was open, I had not knocked but instead announced myself with a clear 'hello'. When Biancha turned her head around to greet me, I noticed she had been crying, and Felicity still was.

'Oh, is this a bad moment? I can come back another time.'

Mark spoke up. 'No, no! Ophelia's waiting for me at the church. I'm on my way out. I'm sure Felicity will appreciate your company. You're family, my dear.'

He spoke those words with a degree of emotion. I felt very confused. As he left the room, I walked towards Felicity.

'I should go. I'll come back later and stay for the night,' Biancha said.

'No, B. I need both of you here.'

I could no longer contain my curiosity. 'What's going on?'

'Can I have a hug?'

'Of course!'

She stretched her arms towards me, and I sat on her bed and hugged her. She started crying again, and I just waited and began to stroke her forehead very gently with the side of my index finger.

Eventually, Felicity explained that she had managed to get her dad to speak about Felix, especially about the day he died. I heard Biancha sobbing and placed my hand on her shoulder offering some comfort.

'Guys, I'm all for showing emotions so don't be shy. It really doesn't bother me. Having said that, I feel this is YOUR time, as sisters. This is about "siblinghood", to coin a term. You should be together.'

'Thanks, Clarissa. I'd like to grab some food but I won't be long. If you could stay with Flic while I dash out to the cafe?'

'Of course. Go home and shower, if you like. I'm not in a rush.'

'Do I smell that bad?'

The three of us laughed and Biancha left. Felicity grabbed my hands. 'I'm so glad you're in my life. Thank you.'

'You're welcome, Fli. But it wasn't my decision to meet you. The universe did that.'

'I know. But it was your decision to stay. And I'm also thankful for that.'

'Likewise. So how's the treatment? Have the doctors said anything about your progress?'

She told me the doctors sounded positive and that there were only two more chemo sessions to go. All being well, she'd be home for her birthday. And mine.

'You look a bit restless.'

'Yeah, the conversation with Dad and Biancha was very intense. I finally know what happened the morning he died. I can't handle going over it now, so I'll tell you another time.'

'No pressure from me. If you don't ever want to tell me, it is okay too.'

'I do wanna tell you. Just not now.' She took a deep breath, looked down and went on.

'Did you get my letter?'

'Which letter?'

'Oh it was nothing. Probably got lost in the mail. It was just a card I made with the kids. Before the op. And I added a few lines on a separate sheet of paper.'

'I didn't. I would've told you. Especially if the kids were involved.'

'I'm sure you would. I just thought, because it was weeks ago, that maybe you got it while I was in the ICU and then by the time you had a chance to talk to me properly, you may have forgotten. When I Face-Timed the kids yesterday they asked me if you had received it so I thought I'd ask you.'

'I hope you remember what was in the card so I can thank them eventually. Luckily, they haven't mentioned anything to me. Better that they believe I got it.'

She started to blink and open her eyes wide.

'Are you okay?'

She slurred a bit. 'I'm okay, I'm just, yeah, it's foggy hey?'

She opened her eyes wider again, then her torso fell forwards, leaning against me. I tried speaking to her and shook her a bit then I panicked and started calling the nurse. I pushed the emergency button and shouted at the same time, 'Help! Nurse! Emergency! Help!'

As a nurse came in, I explained she was unconscious.

'How long has she been like that?'

'It just happened. She was speaking then I noticed she was blinking, and she said it was foggy.'

The nurse started talking to Felicity. 'Can you hear me? Can you nod or blink if you hear me?' As there was no response, she proceeded to put an oxygen mask on Felicity. Another nurse walked in and looked at me.

'Are you okay?'

'Yes, I am. Please help her. Wake her up.'

'You're shaking. Have a seat.'

'Don't worry about me, just help her.'

I blacked out.

When I regained consciousness, I was in a different room. A nurse was with me. She explained what had happened.

'Your friend's doing fine. You passed out and we had to take you out of the room because we cannot treat visitors in front of a patient. It's just standard procedure. Before I can let you go, I need to make sure you are okay. Is that all right, Ma'am?'

'Yes.'

'Thank you. How many fingers am I holding up?'

'Three.'

'And now?'

'One.'

'Good. Now can you follow my finger with your eyes?' She moved her finger to one side then the other. "Beautiful. Can you look up for me? Now look down. Excellent. You're doing really well. I'd like you to raise your left arm and turn your head to the right at the same time. That's great. Poke your tongue out. Now move it sideways. Good job. I'm going to take your blood pressure now. Is that okay?

'Sure.'

'Can you tell me your full name?'

'Clarissa Torres.'

'That's a beautiful name. Clarissa, what's your date of birth?'

'The seventh of the seventh, nineteen seventy-seven.'

'That's a lot of sevens!' She giggled. 'Do you know today's date?'

'Tenth of June.'

'How old are you?'

'Forty-three.'

'Well done.'

She undid the Velcro® strap of the sphygmomanometer.

'Your blood pressure is a bit low, but not significantly. I suspect you had hypoglycaemia, which combined with your anxiety, as you were fearing for your friend, caused you to faint. Have you eaten recently?'

"Not for a few hours.'

'I'm going to get you a light snack, just to help you with the level of sugar in your blood. Make sure you eat a proper meal later on, okay?'

'That's very kind. Thank you.'

'You're welcome. Do you have any questions?'

'Yes. Was I gone for long? And did anyone tell Felicity what happened?'

'Not at all. You were unconscious for a couple of minutes at the most. My colleague has told me Felicity woke up and is doing fine. We're in the room next to hers so you can see her soon.'

I was given a box of fruit juice and some packed crackers with cheese. I ate it quickly then walked to the restroom. I looked at myself in the mirror, splashed some water on my face and dried it with a paper towel. When I returned to Felicity's bedroom, she was sitting up.

'I'm sorry. I hope I didn't scare you too much.'

'Don't be silly. All good. I was fine,' I lied.

Biancha arrived shortly after. I stayed just for a few minutes to make sure she was okay, then I left.

CHAPTER 18

A LETTER,
A DREAM,
A STORY

The following day my boys had an important event at school, and I had full day of professional development ahead. Parts of it were interesting, parts were dull. I particularly liked one session that explored Freud's theory of 'The Protective Shield against Stimuli' and its relevance in today's western society. I did not manage to visit Felicity that day but I rang her at night. She sounded well but had her mum with her in the room, so we didn't speak much. I remember feeling more tired than usual, so I had an early night. In the morning, I felt terrible and not long after, I suspected I had the flu. That meant I could not go anywhere near Felicity until all the symptoms were gone. I got a Covid-19 test done just to be sure.

I asked Biancha to update me on anything important and exchanged text messages with Felicity. A few times during the week we video-called too. When I finally felt I had made a full recovery, I returned to work. It was a Thursday. Generally, I would stop by the hospital before work, but I feared I might still be contagious.

There was a work function I had completely forgotten about the following day. I decided to go, as I hadn't been out in a long time. It's often appealing to have access to free drinks and finger food. The music wasn't too bad either.

A colleague had introduced me to a friend at the conference I attended just before I got sick. She had been invited to our function as a guest from her agency, which had a partnership with ours. Her name was Michelle. At the conference, we had a coffee together but with a few other people. Now it was just the two of us.

'Chris told me you also work at the correction centre.'

'That's right. You do some work there too?'

'Our agency has a contract with the centre, but I don't work there myself. I go there very occasionally.'

'Right.'

We kept chatting for the best part of the night while we were there. She was very attractive, assertive, and sounded educated. I guessed she was about my age, and looked a lot more athletic than me.

'You go to the gym often?'

'I do. I have a gym at home.'

'Nice.'

'What about you?'

'I don't go to any gym.'

'You look fit.'

'Thanks. You're kind.'

'It's the truth. How d'you do it? Cycle to work? What's your secret?'

'I try to eat healthy, and I run.'

'I like running too. Where d'you go? I'm assuming you don't use a treadmill'

'Sometimes King's Park, sometimes another park near home.'

'Nice. You live far?'

'Shenton Park. You?'

'I actually live quite far. Near York. But I've booked accommodation for the weekend. In Wembley.'

'That's handy.'

As the conversation progressed, she managed to let me know she was not straight AND that she was single. I was certain Chris had told her about me. I didn't really mind, but thought it would have been nice if he'd at least warned me.

When I'd had enough, I said goodbye to the people I knew and started making my way out. Michelle followed me. She said she didn't want to lose contact and asked if she could have my number. As she noticed my reluctance, she offered me one of her cards.

'Here. If you feel like it, you text me.'

'Thanks.'

'Can I drive you home? Wembley isn't that far from you.'

I didn't want her to see where I lived so I asked her to drop me off at the Shenton Park IGA, which was open 24 hours, and I pretended I needed to grab a few things. She took me there and said if I wanted, she'd wait for me, but I declined the offer. Then she got out of the car, opened my door and waited for me to get out. It was a foggy night and that reminded me of Felicity's fainting. As we were saying goodbye, she kissed me. We stayed there engaged in that action for a few seconds, until the image of Felicity suddenly came to my mind. I pulled away and gasped.

'What's wrong?'

'I'm sorry. I can't do this.'

'That's okay. It was probably too rushed of me. Sorry. You are too irresistible.'

'It's okay. I must go, though. Thank you for the lift.'

'I hope I see you again.'

'Sure. Bye.'

I turned around before she could say anything else. I went inside the IGA, grabbed a tub of Felicity's favourite ice-cream, Connoisseur Cookies and Cream, paid and made my way out. I decided to walk through the park, as I felt like moving for a bit longer. I saw some young-looking people sitting in the rotunda, talking joyfully and smoking. I could smell marijuana. I remember Felicity telling me about her youth years, and how she had friends who smoked pot regularly and that they'd go to exactly that spot, always after dark. She told me she smoked with them sometimes, just to be part of it.

I walked away from the group, towards the lake. There was no one on the jetty so I stayed there, staring at the lake. I could hear the youngsters laughing and chatting in the background. It was like music, in a way. At some point I noticed a man right behind me. He looked about fifty.

'Evening.'

'Good evening.'

'Sorry to disturb.'

'Not at all. I was just enjoying a bit of fresh air.'

'D'you always bring ice-cream to the park?'

I had completely forgotten that I had the tub of ice-cream in my hands.

'Shivers! I forgot about that. It's probably melted.'

'You can always drink it.' We both laughed. I asked him if he lived nearby.

'No, I don't. But I come here once a year. My little tradition.

'How come?'

'It's because of my best mate's birthday and mine. He passed, you know? We used to come here and kick the ball. Muck around a bit. So my birthday's in August and his is today.'

'That's another Cancer!'

'Cancer? He didn't die of cancer.'

'Sorry. I meant the star sign. 25 June's Cancer.'

'Well, 26th but same, right?'

'Yep. Anyway, I'd better go. I've got to get in the lake.'

'But It's cold. Why would you get in the lake?'

'That's the whole point. We dared each other. I dared him to cross an oval naked in full daylight.'

'And did he?'

'Oh yes. He dared me to cross the lake on the day of his or my birthday. And now I do it every year. I hope he's watching and that it gives him a good laugh. Anyway, how about you? Why are you here?'

'Well, I live very near.'

'And you come here by yourself at some ungodly hour?'

I smiled at him. 'You're funny. No, I don't generally do this. I just wanted some fresh air. I'm trying to get over someone. I went out tonight, had a few drinks, met people, flirted … even had someone chatting me up.'

'Did it work? I mean, did you enjoy yourself?'

'Not really.'

'Still thinking about him?'

'Her.'

'Oh. I beg your pardon.'

'That's okay. Happens ALL the time.'

'It shouldn't, in this day and age. I must get used to saying "they" and stop saying "he" or "she". So you're still thinking about them?'

'Yes, I'm still thinking about her. A lot. I kissed someone else tonight. It was … disgusting. That's why I bought the ice-cream. See if I can get rid of this bad taste. My thought was to have a cigarette. But I don't smoke, you know? And the girl I love, who no longer loves me, is being treated for lung cancer. So the cigarette wasn't a good idea.'

'That's a very sad story. I'm sorry. Sounds like you still like her a lot. Make sure she knows that.'

'Why? What's the point?'

'Loving someone and not telling them is like buying a gift for someone and never giving it to them.'

'She may not want that gift.'

'But you're deciding for her.'

'What if it makes her feel guilty?'

'What if it makes her happy?'

He paused then went on: 'I once made a mistake like that. They assumed I had lost interest. Long story. The short version is it cost my happiness. So I think you should make sure they know. I'm off now. Got a lake to cross. Nice chatting with you. What's your name?'

'Clarissa. What's yours?'

'C J. Nice to meet you. Maybe see you in a year's time. Enjoy your ice-cream.'

I watched as he plodded across the lake. The visibility was low but the sound of his body moving in the water helped. After that I decided to go home. Of course, when I arrived the children were in bed. Leanne was in the lounge watching TV.

'Hi. How's your night?'

'Good. How was yours? Was the function fun?'

'Yeah, it was okay. Were the kids all right?'

'Yep. We played Wii Nintendo after dinner for a bit then they showered and went to bed. They kept a tally and made an agreement: whoever lost would be the first to shower.'

'Typical!' I laughed.

'I'd invite you to watch this with me but you look tired.'

'Yes, It's been a long day. Maybe I'm not completely recovered from the flu yet. Thanks for the thought, though. I should shower and go to bed. Want some ice-cream? It's probably melted but still cold. I thought I wanted some but I'm feeling a bit queasy now.'

'Really? D'you want some medicine? Or I can make you a tea.'

'It's okay, thanks. I'll be fine soon.'

'I'll say yes to that ice-cream.'

She got up and grabbed it from me.

'Enjoy your shower. Oh, there's some mail for you. I left it on the kitchen table.'

I sighed, 'More bills!'

I went straight to my bedroom, undressed and stepped into the bathroom. I stood in front of the mirror for a moment, looking at myself, then I touched my face, from my forehead down to my lips. I opened the tap and scooped some water in my hand, taking it to my lips, trying to clean them. I then washed my whole face, rubbing my hands on my skin and watching my makeup smudge, especially around my eyes. I dried my face with a towel and witnessed it getting slightly wet again, through the two small wells, each symmetrically positioned on either side of the top end of my nose bridge. I closed my eyes and breathed in deeply. I removed my make-up properly with a wet tissue and brushed my teeth. After that, I jumped into the shower. The hot water felt wonderful on my skin. For a moment I forgot about time and just enjoyed the warmth and comfort that came with it. I eventually finished, wrapped one towel around my hair and another one around my body. I walked back to the basin and felt sick, like I wanted to vomit. I tried dry retching to induce it, but nothing much came out. Still, I had a bad taste in my mouth and a terrible sensation in my gut, as well as my chest. I brushed my teeth again and rinsed thoroughly. Not yet satisfied, I brushed them again, this time with no toothpaste. I rinsed my mouth with water and waited. It still tasted foul. I used mouthwash and finally felt better, albeit mentally exhausted. I started to experience shortness of breath, so I sat on the floor and started my deep-breathing exercise. The breathing became better, but tears started puddling under my eyes again.

When I regained control I got up and walked to the boys' room. They looked fast asleep. There were clothes on the floor and some dirty cups on each bedside table. I pulled the blanket over Rupert, who was almost all uncovered, then bent over, getting close enough to smell him, near his face, but making sure I did not touch him so I wouldn't wake him. I did the same with Reuben and felt my heart was warmer and calmer. I collected the cups and got out of their room, making my way to the kitchen, where I grabbed a tumbler and made myself a double gin and tonic with a slice of lime. I added some ice, as I wanted my drink to last longer. I took a sip and thought it tasted just right. As I was leaving the kitchen, I noticed the mail on the table. I looked through the envelopes briefly like a dog sniffing an uninteresting new spot. *As predicted. Bill. Bill. Junk. Bank statement. Junk. Junk. What's this?* A large thick padded plastic envelope was under the other smaller ones. It was from Felicity. I felt my heart pounding and I froze. *Surely this is more than a card she made with the kids!* I placed my glass on the table and walked to the living room.

'Did the mail come today? Were you here when this arrived? It looks registered,' I asked Leanne.

'Oh yeah, apparently it was delivered to our next-door neighbour's by mistake.'

'When?'

'I'm not too sure. A man knocked on our door today and gave it to me. He said he had a house-sitter for a few weeks because he was away and that when he came back he saw the envelope and realised it was for you. Why? Is it important?'

'I don't think so', I lied, 'I was just surprised. How was the ice-cream?'

'Very tasty. Thank you!'

'Glad to hear. Good night.'

'Night.'

I returned to the kitchen for my drink then went to my bedroom and closed the door. I sat on my bed, turned the lamp on and had another sip of my gin. I opened the envelope and removed the first thing my fingers touched, which was the card the kids had made. There were some stick figures with some captions that said: You, Mum, Rupert, Reuben, Lola, and Me. The 'Me' was obviously Charlie. The two tallest figures, being Felicity and me, were each holding a wine glass. Hers was clear and mine had a red drink in, an accurate representation of our drinks of choice. There was also a big love heart. I smiled and thought about how much I loved them. Inside the card, there was a more elaborate drawing of a landscape with the sun, some flowers and a lake or some sort of pool. I was still smiling when I closed the card and placed it next to me, on my bed. I then pulled the next item that my hand found inside the envelope. As my eyes read the first line, I started crying again. It said, 'Last Will and Testament of Felicity Merz'.

She was leaving me as the guardian of her children, had organised a trust with financial arrangements for them, and wanted me to live in their house if she did not survive the treatment.

Next, I pulled out a hand-written letter:

* * * * *

Shenton Park, May 2021

My Clarissa,

I am so sorry for all the pain I have caused you. I know I apologised to you that night at my place. But since I was drunk, I feel you deserve an official apology, from a more sober me.

I am so sorry I took you for granted and that I allowed my weakness to take over, and I subjected my most pure emotion to its peril. I have no words and no excuse for it, except to say I truly regret it.

If I survive and am able to live a healthy life again, I shall try to prove to you that I do love you so much. I always have, and always will. As I sit through this process of healing, I am faced with the possibility of the end. My greatest fears are the welfare of my children and everything left unsaid, especially to you. It's like I fear I'm out of time to say all I want, much of which was hidden, locked away and almost lost, in some remote corner of my soul. It's strange how I spent so much time scared of words, scared of allowing them out, scared they could harm me and my loved ones. Now I'm terrified of having to go before I'm able to set them free, able to utter every single one of them. That's why I need you to know what and how I really feel about you.

I've been lying to you. It is not true that I don't want to be in a relationship. Well, I don't, unless It's with you. In fact I cannot think of a time that I did not want to be with you, ever since we were committed. It is also not true that I feel no desire. Every time I see you I have to make a phenomenal effort not to kiss you, which did not work at my daughter's birthday party, by the way.

I've tried to encourage you to start dating someone else mainly for two reasons: first because I want you to be happy. Second because I'm scared of causing you any more pain. I've harmed you enough. I feel that I can only allow myself to be with you if the shadow of death is no longer around, or at least not so close. Because if we were together now, and I didn't survive my operation, for instance, I'd be abandoning you, and letting you down again. And my wish for you to be happy is far greater than my fear, and ache, of the risk of you finding a new partner, and me staying alive, without you.

However, I don't want to die and leave you believing my love for you is gone. It is not. If anything, It's only grown.

I have learned so much over the past 20 odd months. Even the pandemic has taught me something, to be more economical with the company I keep, and to care less about people's opinions. With the imposition of social distancing and less socialisation, I learned that I don't need to invite people to parties just to please everyone. And I learned that I need to be polite and courteous first to myself and to the ones closer to me. For the past two years I have missed you so much that I feel one of my arms has been amputated, literally. I have a recurrent nightmare, in which I'm lost in the woods at night, and I can't walk or move for some reason, then I see you behind a tree, but all I really see is your arm, but I know it's you. That's when I realise, in my dream, that my own arm's missing. Then just before I can reach your arm, with my left hand, a cat mews and that's when I wake up.

Do you still love me? Are you still in love? If so, and if I survive in good health, I'd like you to marry me. I'd propose to you now, but I don't have the right to do that, not while my life is walking on a tight rope. My soul won't rest if I leave you widowed so early. And this is why we must remain in the friendship zone.

Life is rehearsing to bid farewell and death is inviting to kiss me. I'm rejecting both and I promise I'll fight with all my strength.

I hope, regardless of whether your feelings for me have died or not, that you can believe in everything I say, and that you can find forgiveness inside yourself. I am trying to forgive myself for breaking your heart, like Leanne said to me, and for breaking us.

I'm sorry, my love.

Please be happy, and if I need to go, teach our kids to be happy. I'll be forever grateful for having met you and am a better person because of you. It's only because of all I learned with you that I am able to face all my demons from the past, and make peace.

Forever yours,
Felicity

* * * * *

I had to pause my reading a few times to catch my breath. I finally reached the end of it, feeling overwhelmed. I decided to read it again, and again. Eventually, I folded it and placed it back in the envelope. I grabbed my glass to have another sip and realised it was empty. I got up and filled it with water then drank.

I lay in bed and tossed for a while. I closed my eyes and tried to think of nothing, but I failed in my attempt. I gave up on trying to sleep, got changed and left for a run. I reached the park in a few minutes then kept running around the lake. This time I was not listening to music, which was unusual.

Instead, I was listening to Felicity's voice inside my head, the words from the letter echoing repeatedly. 'I've been lying.' 'It's not true I have no desire.'

The more I heard the words, the worse I felt. I am not sure if I was sad or angry. It was like being lost in a maze, and the sense of desperation that comes with not finding one's way out. I kept running and by now was sweating a lot. When my body could no longer accept the demands of my brain, I slowed down and walked for a bit. It was still dark, as it wasn't even 6 o'clock yet, according to my watch. I sat on the grass by a horizontal log that I often used as a bench. I pulled up the hood of my jumper to cover my head then lay down looking up, searching for stars. I nodded off and had a dream about Dominique. I was sitting on that very log and experiencing a lot of pain. I was bleeding and Dominique started stitching my open wounds, one by one, until she moved onto my back and began to stitch my wings back. The thread was magical in its therapeutic properties. It felt cold at first, which helped numb the pain. 'Can you stitch Felicity's surgery cut with your thread?'

'No, sorry. But you can. I'm going to leave some extra thread for you. Once it reaches your heart, it will be ready for you to use on her. Right now it's only good for your own wounds.'

'Why is it hurting more now?'

'Because it gets worse before it gets better. And maybe because some people don't know how to cry for help.'

Then I heard a cat meow and woke up. The sun had risen and was shining in my face. I cast my memory back in an effort to make sense of the moment then I remembered isolated parts of the night before: the image of Michelle kissing me was at the forefront, then I had a recollection of Felicity's letter.

As the meowing continued, I remembered my dream. I sat up, scanned the area and tried to establish where the sound was coming from. When I saw a kitten trapped in a tree, I got up and walked towards it and saw that it was black. At least it wasn't crossing a road, so I didn't have to fear bad luck.

'Hello. What's your name? Where's your mama?'

I looked around the area for any sign of another cat. I wasn't sure if it was a stray. I wanted to help it but I thought it might bite me. As it kept meowing, I thought about my dream again. "Some people don't know how to cry for help."

'You're crying for help, aren't you? You wouldn't bite me, would you?'

I started to get closer to the kitten very gently. I covered my hand with the end of my jumper sleeve just to be safe, and got close enough until I was touching it. As I attempted to stroke it, it let me. I moved my other hand, also with gentle movements. When I felt I had gained its trust, I picked it up. The cat came without resistance.

I placed it on the ground.

'There you go. Where d'you live? D'you remember the way back?'

I looked sideways, checking if there was anyone that looked remotely like they were looking for a lost pet. The park was almost deserted. I knelt down and patted it a bit and suddenly realised its front paws were white.

'You're like Snowpaws. Oh my goodness. I wish Felicity could see you.'

I wanted to take a photo of Snowpaws II, but realised I didn't have my phone on me. I assumed I had left it home.

I patted the cat again and sat down. I thought about my dream, I thought about Felicity's nightmare, and Domi's reading of my coffee cup. Snowpaws climbed onto my lap. My head was spinning. I didn't know if I was hungover or just tired, but I started to develop a feeling of anxiety, like I had to see Felicity as soon as possible. I had flashbacks of our conversation at her house the previous month—'We waste so much time with unimportant things'—the image of her wardrobe drawer with my clothes, and her Will, which was the scariest of all those memories, as it smelled of death, and I wanted us to live.

It's about 1.5 kilometres from the park to the hospital, so I gave in to my urge and started walking there, kitten in arms. I don't know what I was thinking—I actually was not. Needless to say, I wasn't allowed in with a cat. I realised my stupidity straight away. I really wanted to see Felicity, so the closest thing right then was a phone call, except that I remembered I didn't have my phone on me. I could have asked to ring her from the front reception but the fact I was carrying a cat restricted my access to the building. I left Sir Charles Gairdner Hospital and walked home as fast as I could. The kids were up and happy to see me and noticed the cat straight away.

'You got us a cat?' Rupert asked enthusiastically. I let him hold it.

'I've named it Snowpaws, after Fli's old cat. D'you like it?'

'Are you serious? We can keep him?'

'Well, we'll look after it for now. If we discover it has a home already, we'll have to return it. But I have a feeling it'll be ours.'

'Hi Snowpaws. How are you?'

'Have you boys had breakfast?'

'Not yet, Mum.'

'How about we have some? I'll have to go out soon and spend some time with Felicity. I promise we'll do something fun later on.'

'Sure, Mum.'

'Where's Leanne?'

'She's in the backyard.'

'I need to speak with her. I'm thinking I'll leave some money with her and you guys can walk to the shops and get some food for Snowpaws.'

'Could we go to the pet shop?'

'You could. I was thinking we should take it to the vet next week and when we do that, we can visit the pet shop properly.'

'Mum, stop calling him "it". He's a boy.'

'Sorry, you're right.'

I left the boys with Snowpaws and walked to the backyard to speak with Leanne, checking if she could stay with the boys for a few hours.

'I'll be home until 5 so that's fine.'

'Thank you so much. And … do you mind cats?'

'That's random. No, I don't. Why?'

'I brought a cat home. A kitten, actually.'

She laughed.

Can I give you some money so later the boys can buy some cat food? I'm happy for them to go alone but feel free to join them if you wish.

'Sure, no worries. I was going to the shops anyway.'

'Cool. I'll leave the money on the coffee table.'

'Sure.'

I went back inside, washed my hands, asked the boys to do the same, then the three of us prepared breakfast. I decided to have a toast with jam, Reuben wanted a soft-boiled egg and toast, and Rupert chose to have crumpets.

'May I have some ice-cream, Mum? Please?'

'Well, Since it's Saturday, I'll let you have some.'

'That's not fair,' said Reuben. 'I want some too!'

'You can both have some.'

Rupert opened the freezer to grab the ice-cream.

'Mum, your phone's in the freezer!'

'What?'

'Here.'

Both of them laughed and looked at me inquisitively.

'Well …What can I say? Maybe I'm sleepwalking these days…'

I touched the phone but it did not respond. It was frozen. Literally.

'Fuck!'

'MUM!'

'Sorry guys.'

They laughed again. Snowpaws was meowing by Rupert's foot.

'He's hungry. May I give him some milk?'

'Milk's not actually good for them. Give him some of my oat milk.'

'Okay.'

Snowpaws seemed to like the oat milk and drank it all up. We finished eating our breakfast, and I excused myself and went straight to the shower. I needed to make sure I wouldn't pass on cat hair or fleas or any harmful bacteria to Felicity.

I needed to see Felicity and speak with her. I wanted to rehearse my lines, or at least my initial line, but I had some kind of a mental blank and was not at all sure of what words I'd say. It was like the words I were looking for did not exist. As if what I was feeling, and the message I wanted to transmit, were beyond the abstract.

I put on my clothes, choosing a top Felicity had given me a long time ago, and combed my hair in front of the mirror. I was still hoping to be able to draft my opening line, yet nothing of substance came to me. I brushed my teeth, grabbed my bag and went to say bye to the boys and Leanne. After that, I slid my hand into my handbag looking for my car key. As I didn't find it, I went back to my room and checked the pockets of the clothes I'd been wearing. Nothing there either. So I decided to leave on foot.

As I arrived at the hospital, I made my way to Felicity's room. Except she wasn't there. I went to the reception counter and was told she had been discharged. I was both relieved and frustrated at the same time. I wondered whose place she'd been taken to. I decided to try hers first. My urge to see her started to escalate as I walked back from Nedlands towards Shenton Park. By the time I reached the north side of Aberdare Road, I had started to run. I glanced at my watch. It was 10:30. In about ten minutes, I arrived at Felicity's house. Biancha's red Volkswagen was parked on the driveway and the front door was open. I walked in with no hesitation and saw Biancha, who smiled and greeted me.

'Hi. So good to see you! Flic'll be delighted. She's in the loo. Do you ever answer your phone?'

I was a bit out of breath and did my best to reply.

'Hi B. Mmm, did you ring me? Sorry I missed your call.'

'We rang you a few times. Anyway, I take it you're better? Flic said it was the flu that you had last week, not just a cold.?'

'Yeah, I'm okay now. Listen, I'm sorry to be so blunt but ...'

'But?'

I took a deep breath and exhaled.

'Is Fli okay? Is she staying home?'

'Yes. She's okay. I'll stay here with her and the kids are coming at dinner time.'

'I need to be alone with her. Is that possible?'

'Absolutely! In fact I just remembered I left a turkey in the oven.' She giggled and I chuckled and thanked her. Felicity walked into the lounge.'

'Hi lady! What a surprise?'

Biancha was the next to speak: 'Flic, Mum just rang me. She needs me to help her with something. Will you be okay with Clarissa for a while? I'll come back later.'

'So long as Clarissa's free.'

'I'm free.'

'Cool, I'd better go. Clarissa, could you take care of Flic's suitcase?'

'I can take care of my own suitcase, you clowns! It's on wheels.'

Biancha left, Felicity grabbed the handle of the suitcase and started walking towards her bedroom.

'Come with me. I wanna tell you about my plans for my birthday.'

I followed her. As we entered the room, she abandoned her luggage by the bed and walked towards the window. She drew the curtains open then turned around to face me and gave two steps forward. I had an odd feeling in my stomach, as if there was a block of ice in it. She smiled at me as I stared at her and started moving in her direction.

'I hope you're feeling better. From the flu.'

I nodded gently and kept walking towards her.

'Are you okay?'

I nodded again but wasn't able to utter any word. I got close enough to her so I stopped. One more step and our bodies would touch.

'Clarissa, what are you doing?'

My feet stayed anchored to the floor but my head moved slowly towards hers. Felicity involuntarily moved her own head backwards. As I kept advancing, she stepped back until one of her heels hit the skirting board.

'Clarissa, what are you doing?'

'Trying to love you.'

'No. Don't. We ... we can't do that.'

By that time I was so close to her that I could feel and smell her breath, which was mixed with mine.

'Why not?' I moved my head a few inches closer to hers.

'Because it's best this way. Best if we don't.'

'It's definitely not the best for me.'

She swallowed and stuttered, 'Well, I, I, I'm f-fri-frigid right now, remember?'

'You're such a bad liar!'

'I am?'

I nodded. 'How about "Every time I see you I have to make a phenomenal effort not to kiss you"?'

Her eyes widened. 'You got my letter?'

I nodded. 'Last night. Technically, this morning. So I'm telling you that it's not the best for me.'

'It's not?'

I shook my head, 'Uh uh. And I don't believe It's the best for you either.'

As she remained silent, our lips locked and we kissed. With our hands intertwined, we made our way to her bed as if we were dancing. She sat on the bed and I knelt down on it, her legs between mine. I touched her face with one hand, caressing her gently, downwards. I unbuttoned her shirt in slow motion, still looking into her eyes, and undressed her torso. I touched her chin and slithered my hand down her neck, towards her left shoulder, across the other one and back. I kissed it and slowly moved up to her ear. She shivered. I moved my lips sideways until they found hers again.

After we finished making love, we remained embraced, our hands clasped together again. I noticed she was breathless.

'Are you okay?'

She nodded.

'Are you sure?'

'Positive.'

'Please tell me if you're not. It's important.'

She kissed me and whispered, 'Darling, I'm still going. Don't talk now.'

She closed her eyes and moved her chin up gently. She whispered again, 'Oh God.'

'What?'

'I saw stars!'

'Are you sure you're okay?'

'Fuck, yeah!'

I burst into laughter. She grinned at me and asked, 'Did you see them too?'

I shook my head and continued laughing. She laughed too, rested her head on my chest and started playing with my hair until we both nodded off. When I woke up to go to the toilet, my movement woke her, as she was still resting on me. I spoke very softly, 'Sorry to wake you.' She smiled.

As I returned, she was under the blanket. I joined her but propped my head up a bit by placing a cushion on top of my pillow.

She spoke first. 'I love your tattoo.'

'Really?'

'Yes. How've you been?'

'Apart from the flu, and last night, yeah.'

'What happened last night?'

'Well, it was a crazy night. Not very eventful. It was more in my head. I was going home from a function and got dropped off at the IGA, then I stopped at the park.'

'And then?'

So I told her about the conversation with CJ, the man who crossed the lake, leaving out the bits about Michelle and I kissing.

Felicity sat up.

'How old was he?'

I shrugged. Could be about my age. Not that much older. Why?

'I think that was Connor.'

'Are you serious?'

'A hundred per cent. Today's Felix's birthday. I didn't know about the lake crossing thing, but I did hear about Felix being suspended for being naked in the school grounds.'

I laughed before I could speak. 'Lucky he didn't get expelled.'

'Well, it was his last year, and he lived there. Shit. All this time, and the poor bastard's still thinking about my brother. Come here.' She pulled me closer.

'You okay?'

'I am. Go on. You were telling me about your night.'

'Oh yes, so he crossed the lake and I walked home, still holding a tub of ice-cream.' It was her turn to laugh.

'Leanne was still up. I no longer felt like ice-cream so I offered it to her. I had a shower, checked on the boys and decided I wanted a gin and tonic. Just as I finished making it, I saw your envelope. I went to my room and read the card, then the Will.' I held her hand and kissed it before continuing with the story. 'And finally your letter, which I read more than once.'

I noticed she was tearful and I noticed my eyes well up too. I tapped the tip of her nose with my index finger. 'You silly girl.'

'I was trying to protect you.'

'From what exactly?'

'Pain.'

I gave a big sigh. 'I understand you now; I'll suffer if you die early. But I need you to understand that I won't suffer any less by not being this close to you. I was okay with the friendship thing because I thought you were no longer interested. But it's a totally different thing knowing you love me. I don't want to waste any time. Not an hour, nor a minute.'

'Me neither. But I'm scared that if I have to go away, you'll be left on your own.'

'Felicity, that would happen whether we are in a relationship or not. For all we know, I could die before you.'

'Unlikely.'

'Yes, but not impossible. Isn't it better to enjoy however much time we have? I thought about this a lot. I couldn't even sleep after I read your letter.'

I told her how I'd walked back to the park with the intention to run and exhaust myself, and how I'd sat down and fallen asleep, about my strange dream and how I woke up with the sound of a cat meowing.

'That's a bit creepy.'

'I know, because of the nightmare you mentioned in your letter.'

'Exactly.'

'Except that …there was actually a cat. A kitten. He was trapped. I wanted to take a photo to show you but I didn't have my phone on me. Anyway, I had this urge to see you. When I rescued the cat and noticed it was black with white paws, my urge to see you got stronger. I was actually feeling anxious. I walked as fast as I could to the hospital.'

I told her I wasn't allowed in with the cat and that I walked back home, ate with the boys, showered and realised I'd misplaced my car key. I also told her Rupert had found my phone in the freezer.

'Did you catch an Uber to the hospital?'

'I walked, only to find you were gone. Then I ran here.'

'You must be exhausted. I'm sorry.'

'It was all worth it.'

'Hey, I won't be driving for a while. Why don't you take my car for now?'

'I'm not sure about that. Your car's so fancy. I don't even have a locked garage.'

'Doesn't matter. It's only till you find your keys.'

'Well let's see how it goes. I won't take your car today but if I need to go somewhere, I might ask you.'

'Okay.'

'And thank you.'

She smiled at me, I smiled back and we cuddled.

'Anyway, back to my saga. I considered ringing you from the hospital's payphone, but the truth is I had so much to tell you but I also felt I had no words to express what I wanted. I also felt that whatever I had to communicate had to be done face to face.'

She looked pensive and spoke. 'That's what Felix said.'

'What?'

'Never mind. I'll get to that later. Then what?'

'Well then … you saw the rest. Here we are.'

'Are you feeling better? I mean about the anxiety?'

'Of course. You need to ask?'

'Just checking. I don't want to guess.'

'How about you?'

'Well I'm … still a bit scared, a bit raw, but elated to have you in my arms.'

'Likewise.'

'There's something I'd like to share with you. Can you handle it now? It's about Felix.'

'Of course.'

'Can you get my suitcase on the bed? I need something from it.'

I grabbed her suitcase; she opened it and removed a box from inside it. I took the suitcase away so as to free up space on the bed. She opened the box and removed a hardcover journal. On the first page it had a few words: 'To my dearest Felicity. This is just one more example of something empty that you can improve by filling it. You can choose words or images. Merry Christmas. Felix.'

'Dad found this when Felix's body was … discovered. There were a few other things on his bed. I believe he intended for all of them to be seen.'

I nodded, encouraging her to go on.

'I'm going to tell you what I found out about Felix's death. What most likely led to it.'

'Okay.'

'It turns out that while I was at the scouts' club, Dad took Felix to some woods to help him find a Christmas tree.

Felix wouldn't shut up about Connor, either just talking about him, or asking if Dad had heard any news, received any phone calls, which might explain why he had not arrived yet in Perth.

'What Dad had never told anyone was that Connor's dad had rung him, back in November, basically to say he was aware the two boys were planning to run away together. He said to Dad that he was going to delay Connor's arrival by spending Christmas with Connor and the rest of the family in Melbourne. He wanted Dad to send Felix away at the beginning of January, so it would be safe for Connor to spend some time in Perth. The problem was that Felix did not want to go to university. Dad had told him to do a short course or an apprenticeship and that he'd continue to pay for his accommodation and other costs, but it was better if he stayed over east for a bit longer. Felix said he'd do a Certificate III, but that he would not promise more than that.'

She continued. 'When Anthony rang Dad, he said that he was trying to sort things out in a civilised way, but since Felix had now turned eighteen, he could be charged with a crime if it was found that he had committed one. Connor was still seventeen. Then he reminded Dad that sexual intercourse between two men was not legal unless both parties were of legal age. "If your son seduces my son, I'll have no choice but to involve the police."

'Dad told me that in his desperation, he made a very bad decision that day.'

Felicity started crying again and wasn't able to speak for a while. I just waited and caressed the back of her head, cuddling her again.

'Sweetheart, you don't have to tell me.'

'I want to tell you. I want you to know. I NEED you to know.'

'Okay. Then I want to know too. But it doesn't have to be now. It doesn't have to be today. Just have a rest. Breathe.'

'It's okay. I can do this. Just allow me to be sad because it's a sad topic.'

'Of course. I will hold this space for you. For as long as you need. I just worry about your health but if you want to keep talking, I'm listening.'

So she told me the rest of the story. Apparently, that morning, in December 1993, Mark was feeling very frustrated. He remembers it as a very hot day, flies buzzing around and landing on their faces, on and off. At some stage, Felix informed Mark that he had no intention of going over east. That he had considered it but with Connor missing, he was determined to stay until he found out where Connor was.

Fearing seeing his son going to gaol and also the possibility of the two boys running away, Mark felt desperate and thought he needed to do something. Felix kept talking about Connor until Mark reached the limit of his patience, held Felix's shoulders and said in a very firm tone. 'Son, you need to move on with your life.'

'What d'you mean?'

'Connor's not coming back. You must forget him.'

'Of course he's coming back! Why wouldn't he?'

'Because he's dead!'

'What?'

'That's right. He's died. That's the reason the whole family's away. There was an accident.'

Felix dropped everything he was holding and ran away.

Mark couldn't find him despite looking for a long time, first on foot, then by car. By the time Mark got home, Felix was dead.

CHAPTER 19

FELIX'S MESSAGE

When Felicity finished, the poignancy had permeated the whole room and started infiltrating my cells. I looked at all the characters of that family and saw the tragedy that had been hidden, disguised, but also dragged for nearly three decades. I thought about the legacy that Lacan, the noted psychoanalyst, talks about, and how I had chosen to totally reject mine. First, I felt lucky. Then I felt that was not luck. I realised it was my own way of hiding and disguising and dragging.

I waited for Felicity to calm down. Neither of us spoke for a few minutes, although we both were crying. I wrapped my arms around her and held her tight, hoping that she would feel emotionally contained. When she was no longer sobbing, she sighed deeply.

'Fli, this was already a sad story but it got way sadder.'

'Well, there's more.'

She wiped the tears off her face with a tissue, blew her nose, took a deep breath and licked her upper lip gently, from one side to the other. She pointed to the box and said that it contained other items that were found on Felix's bed the day he died: his Bible, an open pack of cigarettes, a matchstick box, two t-shirts that were almost identical, but had been made up with each other's half. Felix cut his own t-shirt in half, a vertical cut on each side, and did the same with one of Connor's t-shirts. Then he sewed the back of one with the front of the other, and vice-versa. Felicity says she recognised Connor's, because Felix liked wearing it to bed.

She showed me the two t-shirts and smiled. She grabbed one and held it close to her face, smelling it, then placing it on the bed. She proceeded to grab the Bible. She opened it and removed a loose page.

'This is a message Felix left for Connor.' She handed me the loose page and I looked at it. On top, it said, 'To: Connor', written by hand. It was a page from the Book of Second John. Verse 12 was highlighted:

'Having many things to write unto you, I would not write with paper and ink: but I trust to come unto you, and speak face to face, that our joy may be full.'

(2 John 1:12)

Again, I could not contain my tears. I closed my eyes, sighed and hugged her again.

'So, I've decided to contact Connor.'

'And have you found him already?'

'I have his address. But I haven't acted on it yet. I wrote a letter, which I'd love you to read some other time and let me know what you think. I'd like to give him one of the t-shirts, the page from the Bible, and tell him the real reason my brother ended his life. For the time being, I'd like you to look after this box for me. If everything goes well with my health, then I'll make arrangements to meet Connor, and I'd like you to join me. If things don't go so well, I'd like you to contact him. The address is on the envelope anyway.'

'Okay sweetheart. Thank you for sharing all this with me.'

'There's only one more … little thing.'

'Yes?'

'I told Dad. About you. After he told me the events of my brother's last hours with him.'

'What did you say?'

'I said, "Dad, Clarissa is my Connor. Unlike Felix, I hope I live to share my life with her."'

'Wow.' We were both silent for a moment, then I spoke. 'And did he say anything?

'Yes. He said, "I hope you live too, my dear. And I wish Felix was here too. I know you think I was ashamed of him. You said that many times. And I can't blame you. But what I want you to know is that all these years, I've been ashamed of no one but myself." And that was pretty much when you arrived.'

'No wonder you fainted that day. So you haven't told your mum then?'

'Nope. It's not that I planned it. It's just the way it happened.'

'Funny.'

'Why?'

'I was just thinking. I don't think he's told your mum either.'

'Biancha says the same. But why? What makes you think that?'

'I just overheard her, nothing serious. She sounded pleased you were no longer dating a woman. Something like that.'

'I see. Ummm. Well that's too bad because now I am.' She smiled again and I saw her joy. It went straight to my heart.

We lay down and decided to have a snooze. I asked her to set her alarm for 3 pm in case we overslept, as I remembered Leanne was leaving at 5. We slept holding each other and woke up to the unpleasant sound of the alarm.

I showered and put my clothes back on. She suggested I come back later but I told her that because this was her first night with the kids since her treatment had started, it may be better for her to be just with them. 'if I came back,

I'd need to bring my boys. I think it'd be great for them to be just with you and Biancha.' She agreed. I promised to visit her the following day. She called Biancha and said I was leaving shortly. The doctors had recommended that Felicity was not left alone, at least for the first few weeks. Biancha brought the children with her. They ran towards Felicity and covered her in kisses and hugs.

And so I left, unable to stop playing the movie of Felix's last day of his life inside my head. A very short movie, I'll admit. But it was a very short life too.

On Sunday morning, I took the boys to their soccer game. It was pouring so it wasn't the nicest of experiences, at least for the adults, although the kids seemed to be having fun. After the game, which luckily was at Rosalie Park, we went home to get changed and I took them out for pancakes, something we hadn't done in a while. On our way back they asked to stop at the park.

'Where did you find Snowpaws, Mum?'

'I'll show you.' So I walked towards my favourite spot, where the log is, and pointed to the tree. They ran towards it and climbed it. 'Join us, Mum' So I did. Going up was easy. The hard bit for me was to get down. In the end I just grabbed hold of a branch, hung from it, and jumped to the ground. The boys wanted to play for a bit longer, so I waited on the log. They started hanging from a branch and jumping to the ground. Then they decided to do it in synch and asked me to record them.

'Sorry guys, Mum's phone isn't working really well. I'm going to have it sorted this afternoon.'

They went on playing regardless, and asked me to be the one counting to three so they'd jump together. They said they wanted to come back another time so I could video record them in slow motion. At some point, Reuben squatted, grabbed something from the ground and announced, 'Mum! I think this is our car key.'

I got up and walked towards him. He was right. It was our key.

'Reuben, you're so wonderful! This'll save me so much hassle!'

Rupert protested: 'I found your phone.'

'Yes, darling. You are also wonderful!'

'I'm more wonderful, Rupert. The key's undamaged. You found a broken phone.'

'I still saved her time. She could still be looking for the phone. And she'd only lost it for a few hours. It took you a whole extra day to find the key.'

I decided to divert their attention, so they'd put an end to their little competition. 'Guys, now that we can drive, how about we go to the pet shop?' It worked. We went to City Farmers, where I let them choose a collar, bowl, a bed, the little toilet tray and a few toys for Snowpaws.

'When can we show Snowpaws to Lola and Charlie, Mum?'

'Well, next time they come here. We must be careful though.'

'Why?'

'Felicity is very vulnerable now. I mean her health. She wants to meet Snowpaws too but just a bit of cat hair could make her unwell. So I'd rather wait till we take Snowpaws to the vet, take care of possible fleas, then Lola and Charlie can meet the new member of the family.'

On Monday our state government announced there'd be a lockdown due to a new case of Covid-19 that had been reported, and restrictions were put into place. Masks became mandatory and people were told to stay home, being allowed to go out only for physical exercise, which had to be outdoors, or for essential work, to buy food, or for medical reasons. Felicity had an appointment scheduled for Tuesday morning, which coincided with her birthday. I had made arrangements to spend Monday night with her, as Biancha had stayed the two previous nights. I decided to keep the boys at home and not send them to school for the rest of the week. They were thrilled. I stayed with them until after dinner and told them they could stay up one extra hour, since they were not going to school.

Felicity was looking well. She invited me for a game of chess. I accepted just to please her, but chess has never been my favourite pastime. I reckon I am good at creating strategies, but chess is very visual. My physical, spatial skills have never been a strength. I know the rules and I can play chess, but that's not enough. Plus I tend to play very defensively, which often results in it taking forever. So I decided to change my strategy and played as aggressively as I could. I still lost.

We went to bed and stayed talking for quite a bit. She decided to change her appointment to a different date, just to avoid going out while there was this threat of the Delta strain of the virus. I am cautious by nature and given her circumstances, thought it was better not to risk it. In the morning, before she woke, I rang the hospital and explained the situation. We were told so long as Felicity was feeling well, the appointment could wait for up to a week.

I made her a tea and prepared some yogurt with berries and muesli, times two, and took it to her bedroom. I left the tray on the bedside table and got under the blankets again. She opened her eyes.

'Happy birthday, my love.'

She smiled, and I kissed her and asked if she was hungry.

'Not very, but I can eat.'

We sat up, ate and kept talking.

'What would you like for your birthday?'

'I don't need anything. Plus, the shops are closed, so you're a bit late,' she said, smiling.

'What makes you think I haven't got your present yet?'

'Well you just asked what I want.'

'I did. But that's the not-surprise present. Then there's the surprise one, which is the one you don't get to choose.'

'Okay. Mmmm, so I think I'd like to see Snowpaws.'

'I can't let you meet him yet. After he's been de-fleaed, vaccinated, and also after we ask the doctors if that's okay.'

'Can't we just google?'

'No. So, think of another thing. Another present.'

'I can't think of anything I really want.'

'Are you sure? I mean, I could give you some stars …'

She chuckled. 'Well hurry up, will you? Where are my stars?'

'Well, let me take care of that.'

Shortly after the stargazing session, while we were just enjoying each other's intimate presence, we heard voices.

'Shit. I think my parents are here.'

'They probably want to wish you a happy birthday.'

'They never come without asking first. This is bizarre.'

'I'd better get dressed.'

'Wait.'

The bedroom door was open, as I had been holding the tray when I walked in and could not close the door. We began to hear the conversation clearer and clearer. It was Ophelia and Biancha. They wanted to surprise Felicity and were decorating the living room.

'Can she eat cake?'

'Yes, Mum. I'm sure she can.'

'I'm thinking of inviting her to my prayer group.'

'Mum, not that again please.'

'I'm worried about her, Biancha. I thought her sexuality moment of confusion had passed. But after what your father told me, I think she needs God.'

'She needs to be left alone, Mum. If you start preaching and upsetting her, I'll be very rude to you, no matter who's present. Especially today. It's her birthday.'

'Maybe we should invite Phillip.'

'Are you out of your fucking mind?' Biancha yelled.

At that moment Felicity sat up.

'Where're you going?'

'I think I need to set a few things straight.'

'Don't allow this to ruin your special day.'

'I won't.'

She got out of bed, threw her silk robe on her naked body, then walked outside. I could not see how close she got to them but as I could hear everything, it was easy to imagine.

'Hi Mum. Good morning B.'

'Felicity! We thought you were at the hospital.'

'Yeah, I figured.'

'This was meant to be a surprise. Happy birthday anyway.'

'Oh, it's been a surprise all right. We're all surprised. The lockdown was a surprise, my last-minute decision to put off my appointment, and this ...visit. Thank you for the thought. And the effort. Now if you excuse me, I'd like to go back to what I was doing. I was having sex, about to climax. Third time this morning. See you later. We're all having dinner together, right? Clarissa's bringing her boys too.'

It was hard to believe my ears. She walked back into the room and saw my face of shock.

'What?'

'Did you really say what I think I heard?'

'Yeah, I think I did.'

We heard the front door close and assumed they had left. Next, we heard the car engine.

'You've lost your mind.'

'On the contrary. I think I've found it! You had to see Mum's face.'

'What about Biancha?'

'You know B. She loved it. She was laughing. I bet she's still laughing her ass off!'

We both laughed. About half an hour later, she received a message from Biancha. 'Ring me when you can'. When Felicity rang Biancha, her phone was on loudspeaker so I could take part in the conversation.

'Hey B, I just want to be prepared for tonight. Does your mum know it's me?'

'She must! She didn't talk about it. Didn't say a word after we left. But I'm pretty sure Dad told her.'

'Honey, if she doesn't know yet, she will tonight. It's great that it's my birthday. I am finally given another opportunity, two years after.'

I had to go home but could not leave until there was someone else to stay with Fli. Mark came over to relieve me. He'd brought the newspapers to keep himself entertained.

CHAPTER 20

THE FIRST SUPPER

I went back home and at about 6pm I was back at Felicity's with the boys. No alcohol was meant to be served. The food looked exquisite, all organised by Biancha.

Felicity was getting ready while everyone waited at the table. When she finally came out of the room, we all yelled, 'Happy birthday!' and her children got up and hugged her. They each had a present for her. She unwrapped each parcel carefully. Lola gave her a bracelet, matching her own, and Charlie gave her a pair of earrings.

'Thank you, my angels. I love them both.'

The three of them walked towards the table.

'Hi B.' Felicity beamed at her sister.

'Hi Flic. How was the rest of your morning?'

'Fanfuckingtastic. Oops! Sorry children.' The kids giggled.

Biancha replied, 'Yeah?'

'Absolutely.'

'Finished what you'd started?'

'Did I what! Even saw stars! My Lord!'

Biancha burst into laughter, covering her mouth with her hand in an attempt to soften it. I wanted to laugh too but felt embarrassed at the same time.

'Shall we eat?'

'Not before we thank the Lord, Mark. I'll do it.'

'No, let me. It's my birthday.'

All the other heads turned to Felicity in disbelief. She started: 'Dear Lord, thank You for this beautiful food. Thank You also for letting me be here with my loved ones. Please keep doing Your work and put some tolerance in the hearts of the intolerant. Help everyone learn to mind their own business and leave others alone. Tell Felix I've started filling up the journal, and also tell him I'm going to visit Connor. Also, help me stay alive and give me the chance to fully experience life as the real me. It's time to do some weeding and get rid of the bad weeds in my life. Lastly, forgive my family for breaking the law and not abiding by our government's rule of self-isolation. They're doing this out of love for me. Please forgive them, Father. They do not know what they're doing. Amen.'

The rest of us said 'Amen' in unison and we started eating. Felicity got up and grabbed a bottle of wine.

'B, can you help me with some glasses?'

Biancha got up and together they got goblets for all of us. She opened the bottled and poured a small serve for everyone, including the kids.

'Don't worry guys. It's non-alcohol wine.'

I saw the relief in Ophelia's face. The kids were giggling. The two sisters went back to their seats and Felicity started clinking her fork against her glass.

Clink, clink, clink. 'I propose a toast. Does anyone want to make a speech?'

Charlie raised his hand.

'This is the happiest day of my life because I was scared my mum may not have a birthday party, and instead she could have had a funeral so I'm happy even though she's bald. To my mum.'

'Thank you, sweetheart.' I saw Felicity use the tip of her index finger to contain the tears.

I raised my glass and said, 'To Charlie's mum.' Everyone joined and echoed me.

Felicity smiled and spoke:

'Anyone else has a speech? Okay. Don't worry, I'm not disappointed. I'll make one, though. I'd like to start by reading a verse from the Bible, from the book of Proverbs. In fact, B, why don't you read it? But only read this particular verse, okay?'

'Absolutely. What is the verse?'

'Proverbs, chapter 31, verse six'

Biancha got the Bible and flicked the pages quickly until she found the Book of Proverbs. Eventually, she read:

'Give strong drink unto him that is ready to perish, and wine unto those that be of heavy hearts'

(Proverbs, 31:6)

Felicity raised her glass and said, 'To wine', and everyone echoed her, the kids giggling. She went on,

'Now I'll read another verse I selected for tonight. B, may I have the Holy Book back?'

Biancha returned the Bible to Felicity.

'I am come into my garden, my sister, my spouse: I have gathered my myrrh with my spice; I have eaten my honeycomb with my honey; I have drunk my wine with my milk: eat, O friends; drink, yea, drink abundantly, O beloved.'

(Song of Solomon, 5:1)

There was a moment of silence. Biancha broke it when she raised her glassed, 'To wine again'

Everyone repeated: 'To wine.'

'And honey and milk, Mummy.'

'Yes, Lola. To wine, honey and milk!'

Everyone raised their goblets again.

'Okay, now my speech, finally. Well, this, luckily, will not be remembered as the last supper. Rather, it's the first! So if any of you betray me for a silver coin or 30, I'll forgive you. However, if I deny knowing the betrayer, on occasion, you must forgive me in turn. So, here's a toast to forgiveness.'

'Mum, you're being so funny,' Lola laughed. Felicity joined her.

'Thank you darling. I love your sense of humour.'

After dinner, we mingled in the lounge. The kids moved to the theatre room and played video games. Felicity was sitting next to me when Ophelia sat on the armchair positioned perpendicular to our seat.

'Mother.'

'Girls! I want to say that I hope you find some clarity soon. I think you're so close, as friends, that you are just a bit confused.'

'Thank you, Mother.'

'You're welcome. I'll keep praying for you.'

'I must admit I am a bit confused. Torn even.'

'It's okay, darling. Trust in the Lord. Tell him everything. He can heal all wounds.'

'I have, Mother. I told him today. I said, God Almighty, why did you not make me grow up as a Jehovah Witness? This way when I left the church, my mother wouldn't be allowed to speak to me.'

Ophelia's semblance changed from showing concern to being stern.

'I love you, Mum, but I won't allow you to interfere in my life choices. You know, I thought you'd learned a bit more when you lost Felix. And the last thing I want to say is this. Please listen very carefully: if I find out that you have said anything, that you have shared any of your twisted thoughts with the children, by the way I mean the FOUR children, I'll have no choice but to keep the kids away from you and your harmful ideas. As for Phillip, I hate to disappoint you but he isn't the great guy you think. He's even signed the papers I asked him to, agreeing to give Clarissa the full custody of the chidden in case I pass away.'

'He wouldn't do that. He's a man of God.'

'Well he has. All I had to do was write a clause saying he'd have no financial responsibility and that any contribution he made would be totally up to him.'

'You're making a mistake, Felicity. Your children have the right to spend time with their father.'

'I've never prevented that, Mother. But I don't want them to live with a man who is not a good role model.'

'He's a man of God. That's a perfect household to grow up in.'

'Mum, Phillip is a drug dealer. You need stop treating him like he's a saint. That's how he makes his money. That's only one of the reasons I left the marriage. So it's not a good household for the kids, no matter how many Bibles you find in his house. Now if you excuse me, I'd like to help myself to some more cake. You coming with me, Honey?'

'I'll join you shortly.'

There was an awkward silence. I saw Ophelia turn her head towards Mark.

'Is it true? About Phillip?'

'I doubt she'd make this up.'

'It's a serious accusation. Why did she never mention it before?'

Mark had no reply to offer. I was the next to speak.

'Ophelia, if you ever wanna talk to me, I'll listen.'

Mark was sitting next to me and patted me on the knee. 'Thank you for everything you've been doing for Felicity.'

'My pleasure. She's done a lot for me too.' I looked at Ophelia and added, 'It's not a matter of us against you.'

'What is it then?'

'I think it's a matter of all of us making an effort to coexist in harmony. And peace. We'll get there.' I smiled and excused myself saying I wanted to have some cake.

All the kids stayed over, as well as me. After they were tucked in, Felicity and I went to her bedroom. I finally gave her my present, which was a ring. She looked at it in awe, then looked at me, and kept shifting her gazer from the ring to my eyes a few times as she spoke:

'Is this …?'

'It is, if you want it to be. And if you don't, then It's just a ring.'

'I want it to be.'

'Okay. Let me do this properly then.' I put some music on, a playlist I had prepared for her, and cleared my throat: 'Felicity Merz, would you like to be my wife?'

She said yes. I put the ring on her finger and kissed her.

In the morning, I waited for Biancha to arrive so that I could go home with my boys. She noticed the ring straight away. I saw her looking at Felicity's finger then at Felicity's face, then at me. She had a smirk stamped on her own face but said nothing. I guessed that was because the kids were present. I left the Merzs together and went home.

I worked from home the rest of the week, and visited Felicity daily, rostering the night-time with Biancha. My birthday was the following Wednesday, so I tried to arrange it in a way that gave Felicity and me some special time but also made sure I enjoyed my kids' company too. It was the school holidays for them. I managed to take another day off. In the morning, the boys brought me breakfast in bed. We watched a movie together, in my bedroom, and finally took Snowpaws to the vet. We went home and played with Snowpaws for a while, then had a late lunch. They gave me a present, which was a coffee grinder. I had to make a coffee now.

I left around 6 pm, partly sad, as I wanted to be with them too, and it was the first time I'd spend the night of my birthday away from them. Felicity's children were still mostly based at their grandparents, as she wasn't fully fit to look after them, with all her medical appointments and health issues. They had also spent the day with her. She'd even ventured out of the house, wearing a mask.

When I arrived, the children were still there. They had baked a cake for me and wished me a happy birthday. I suggested we sing happy birthday and cut the cake.

'Don't you have to eat dinner first?'

'Nuh! It's my birthday and I want to start with the cake!'

They laughed. We sang happy birthday (to me) and ate some cake. They left with Biancha shortly after.

Felicity surprised me with a special dinner, all homemade by her. It was pasta with crab meat, a combination she knew I loved.

'Would you like to watch a movie after dinner?'

'I'd love to!'

We watched *Life of Brian*. I hadn't laughed so much in a long time.

I told her I wanted to have a shower. She said she wanted to ring her dad to discuss something to do with the kids and asked me to wait in the bedroom. When I finished my shower and stepped into the bedroom, the lights were off and there were lots of candles lit. They were battery-operated but that didn't make the scene any less appealing. They were arranged in a trail. The door was open and I saw more candles leading somewhere. I followed the trail, which led me to the stairs. There was one candle on each step, then a few more leading to the threshold of the attic. Felicity was standing by the window.

'I'm glad you found your way.'

'I guess it was easier than for Hansel and Gretel.'

'There isn't a candy house, though. Sorry to disappoint.'

'What are you talking about? This is a gingerbread house, remember?'

She laughed.

'Anyway. I hope you are ready for your present.'

She walked towards me and revealed a small squarish box, which she popped open exposing its content: a ring.

'I had bought this for you before my birthday. You beat me to the question but luckily we're both girls. I get to put a ring on your finger too. So, Clarissa Torres, will you marry me?'

I cried and nodded, and eventually managed to utter a 'yes'. She kissed me and we surrendered our bodies to one another again with passion, until we were so exhausted that we fell asleep. We woke up thirsty in the middle of the night, so I suggested we move to her bedroom and I told her I'd bring water. We fell into slumber again shortly afterwards. Next thing I remember is waking up with a thud. Frightened, I sat up and noticed she wasn't next to me.

'Felicity?'

I heard a moan. I jumped to my feet and saw her on the floor, in the bathroom. I panicked. She was panting.

'Baby, what's wrong?'

She didn't reply. I ran to my phone and rang 000.

'Ambulance. Number 1A King Street, Shenton Park. Please hurry.'

CHAPTER 21

HOPE

I went in the ambulance with the paramedics, but wasn't allowed in the back with her. I rang Biancha, who told me she'd meet me at the hospital. Felicity was taken immediately to the ICU. I wanted to be with her, but as I was crying, the staff persuaded me to wait outside for a bit. Biancha arrived shortly after and I hugged her.

'What happened?'

'I don't know,' was all managed to reply. Then I sobbed.

I don't know how much time went by until a doctor came to speak with us.

'How is she?'

'She's recovering. She's not conscious.'

'So it's that serious?'

'It's an induced coma. Recommended in certain cases so the procedures don't feel as invasive.'

'What's wrong with her?'

'Are you family?'

'I'm her partner.'

'And I'm her sister.'

'Okay. We suspect that your sister has pneumocystis pneumonia,' he said looking at Biancha and ignoring me.

'Okay. I'm not a doctor so can you tell us what that means?'

'It's a fungal type of pneumonia, fairly common in patients with a low immunity system. We've sent a sample to the lab so we're waiting for the results.'

'So what's next?'

'Well, she'll need to be treated. She needs antibiotics and a lot of rest. She has the oxygen mask on at the moment.'

'How serious is it? If it's … this fungal pneumonia?'

'Serious enough, given her condition.'

'Fatal?'

'Not necessarily. But possible. I'm sorry.' He bowed gently and walked away.

I lost control again and wept in Biancha's arms.

'She'll get through this, darling. My sister's resilient. You'll see.'

'You really think so?'

'I know so. She has many reasons to want to live. Seeing stars is just one of them.'

I giggled. 'Thank you.'

I left the hospital and walked home. When I arrived, the kids were in the living room playing.

'Mum, what's wrong? You're crying.'

'Hi guys. I just … Felicity had a relapse and is in hospital again. She'll be okay. I'll be okay too.'

They sat next to me and tried to cheer me up. They showed me some tricks they'd been teaching Snowpaws and I even managed to laugh. I told them I needed to go for a run and that after I'd get us fish and chips. I saw how they 'high-fived' each other.

EPILOGUE

So yes, it's winter. As soon as I stepped out of the house, the air felt cold and sharp, as if penetrating my lungs with rage. Eventually, I'm at the park.

I look up and see a great grey ceiling and get reminded of life as I see a white bird taking flight, swinging her sumptuous wings. I slow down but keep moving. Somehow, I am able to watch that in slow motion, as the dagger pierces my lungs, once, twice, a few times, until I feel there's a rope around my neck, and I'm choking.

I keep thinking about that letter, the words echoing inside my ears, the letters being etched onto my soul, like carvings on ancient rocks. I look at my ring, bring it close to my lips and kiss it.

I just need to make it through one more winter. Then I'll be all right. If the borders open, Dominique may be visiting us for Christmas. Then I'll ask her to patch up my heart and stitch my wings back.

After all, she's a first-aid seamstress.

FELICITY'S LETTER TO CONNOR

Dear Connor,

If this letter was brought to you by someone else and not me, there is a chance I've left this world without the honour and privilege of meeting you again. I'm sure you remember me, Felicity Merz, Felix's younger sister. The lady that has given you this letter, if not me, is my best friend, my soulmate, and the love of my life. I almost lost her completely in trying not to lose what I thought was my reputation and the high regard I wanted others to have for me. It turns out I was losing that from the very person I needed it most: my partner. What has that got to do with you? Well, looking back, I am still in awe of two young lads that were much braver than I've ever been, back almost 30 years ago. Two lads that had more discernment and guts. I'd like my kids to inherit those traits from their uncle.

Thank you for being you and for loving my brother. I don't know much about you, sadly. I don't know what your life was like, I don't know what kind of support you had, nor how long it took you to get over the whole thing. Have you? I want to say that I thought about you often many times during my life. I am sorry I did not reach out earlier. That thought was a bit scary. But it has crossed my mind that you may still feel guilty or somehow responsible for Felix's death. Please, if that is an idea that has been with you, be assured you were not responsible for that. Instead, you were a big part of my brother's self-discovery and exercising of authenticity. The way it ended was tragic and unfair, and I so wish it had not happened, but sill, if the alternative was to repress the beautiful feeling you two shared, that would not have been ok either, and it would have also killed him, inside. It was because of the love you two shared that he was able to wear his identity and essence.

Lastly, I only very recently found out that my brother believed you had died, which is why he took his own life. But he did that out of love, thinking that this would be the only way to see you again. You will understand once you sight the message he left for you, which is enclosed. He was a believer, not a hypocrite. And he was certain that both of you would make it to Heaven. I am certain of that too.

Your and my brother's story is one of the saddest I've known, but also one of the most powerful.

Take care.
Love,
Felicity Merz

AFTERWORD

A new friend of mine asked if I'd let her read any of my writing. She'd been brave and shared one of hers, which I remember had moved me deeply. I then chose the shortest of all my texts, since I have a reputation for writing 'too much', if such a thing actually exists.

Weeks later we met up and shared a coffee. Very apologetically, she told me she had printed my text, and fully intended to read it. However, the title of my story was 'Never Fall in Love with a Cat', and she explained that her own cat had just passed. So she was reluctant to read my story, fearing it would be painful.

I asked her to put that story aside and promised to send a new one. When at home, I went through my files and tried to pick another one for her. Until I came across a file named 'Felicity's Friend', which consisted of one single paragraph. As I read, I remembered writing it, back in mid-2018.

I read the few lines a few times and remembered the two main characters I had started to conceive nearly three years before. *It's time to tell this story*, I found myself saying. So I started, or rather, continued. By the next morning, I had reached three and a half thousand words. The text took a direction I had not predicted, and I was very pleased with it. So I sent it to Mei. After that, I sent it to my best friend in Brazil. Two days later, I found that the story was talking to me, so I started adding to it. I asked both Mei and Dan to refrain from reading. 'Please wait for the full text', I said. They both agreed.

A week later I sent what I believed was the final, complete text, with 10 thousand words to my best friend in Brazil once again. She read it within a couple of days and gave me feedback. As I was extremely pleased with the 'new final version', I decided to send it to Gabi, my translator. 'Would you read this and let me know if you think you'd like to translate it?'

Gabi reassured me she wanted to do the work and hinted at the possibility of me further developing it. 'I think you can explore the relationship between the two characters a bit more. That's the main feeling I got as I finished reading it. There's potential.' I felt flattered but I didn't really want to touch that text so I tried to ignore it. Again, I felt the characters 'talking' to me and eventually I was finding it hard to sleep properly. So I started writing again, and adding to the story. It felt like the characters had a bit more to say.

I was feeling exhausted, because I was still not able to sleep and kept obsessing about the story. Call me schizo if you wish, but the characters were still talking to me! I remember saying, 'What do you want from me?'

Then I had a nap, the day of my birthday, and when I woke up, I felt I had the answer: I needed to come out of the closet as a writer. None of my texts would be of any use if I kept them filed in my computer.

Meanwhile I touched base with Mei, the friend I initially intended to send the story to. She very apologetically again told me her General Manager had read the story, which she had printed and left at work. She said her manager believed that text had been written by Mei, and that it was autobiographical. 'Such a beautiful text! And it must be so hard for you, not being able to be out of the closet'. Coincidentally, the text is partly about sexuality and acceptance, and Mei, identifying as gay, was not, up to that moment, out in her workplace. That reassured me in the sense of exposing myself, my texts. I felt the story had already fulfilled my goal, so yes, I was definitely having it published, even if no one else read it and/or liked it.

I contacted Beverley Streater, with whom I had worked on the *Eighteen Point Five* project, and she was very helpful, from formatting to referencing ,to names of characters. What I am most grateful for is a simple comment she made in relation to one particular scene. She said, 'This could be expanded. If you give more details, it'll become more real. Remember she's his only ally'. I wrote around the scene in question, and it became my favourite scene in the whole story. I suppose I should also thank Gabriela, who was the first to encourage me to further develop the text as a whole.

My final version is about 43,000 words. I believe it is indeed the final version.

Nadja Fernandes, Subiaco, Western Australia 2022

REFERENCES

Barry, J., Greenwich, E. & Spector, P, Be My Baby, in *Be My Baby*, Philles, 1963

Carroll, L., *Alice's Adventures in Wonderland*, Macmillan, 1865

Chaiken, I. & Greenberg, K., *The L Word* Dufferin Gate Productions, Coast Mountain Films, Posse, Showtime Networks & MGM Television, 2004

Brothers Grimm; Browne A. (ill) *Hansel and Gretel*. London; New York, N.Y. Julia MacRae Books, 1981.

Gurvitz, A., Classic in *Classic*, Rak Records, 1982

Ingham, D. et al., *Charlie and Lola* [TV Series]. Adapted from the work of Child L. Kitty Taylor Production Company: Tiger Aspect Productions, BBC Worldwide, 2005

Joel, W. M. (Billy), Piano Man in *Piano Man*, Columbia Records, 1973

Jones, T *Monty Python's Life of Bryan* [Film], John Goldstone, 1979

Kelly, T. & Steinberg, B, True Colors, Recorded by Cyndi Lauper in *True Colors*, Epic, 1986

Michael, G. & Ridgeley, A, Careless Whispers in *Make It Big,* Epic/Columbia/Sony, 1984

Parker, A. *Fame* [Film], David De Silva and Allan Marshal, 1980

Ram, B The Great Pretender in *The Great Pretender*, Mercury, 1955

The Holy Bible: King James Version (KJV). Holman Bible Publishers, Nashville, Tenn.,1979

- 2 John 1:12
- Matthew 5:6
- Proverbs 31:6
- Song of Solomon 5:1